Crash Proof

S.G. Reid

ISBN: 9781983217128

DEDICATION

Dedicated to all of those who are fighting, no matter what your battle. Stay strong. I will not promise you tomorrow will be better, but you will never know unless you wait to watch that sunrise.

Bonus sneak preview
of
Crash Proof – Book 2: Rise from the Ashes
at the back!

Book 1:
Born of the Flames

"The fire which enlightens is the same fire which consumes."
~ Henri Frederic Amiel ~

Chapter 1

Beep...Beep...Beep...

She squeezed her eyes more firmly closed and blocked out the sound. She didn't want to wake up just yet. She didn't want to acknowledge where she was or what was going on. Instead, she kept her eyes closed and let her mind drift.

Beep...Beep...Beep...

The sound kept permeating her thoughts. Swirling her memories from the present deep into the past. To another room where that noise was consistent and equally annoying. She wanted to be in that memory even less than she wanted to be awake.

"Is she going to be alright?"

She remembered herself asking that question over and over again as she sat next to the beeping machine staring down at the pale face in front of her. It had been the first time in years her father had been sober and he'd looked worse for it. He'd spent the whole day in the hospital room's bathroom throwing up. And he hadn't been able to answer her question.

No one had been able to answer her question.

Cooper had sat beside her holding her hand. It seemed like he was always beside her, always attached to her. He hadn't been able to answer her question either, but at least he'd been there. Looking at her intently with his puppy dog brown eyes and waiting for a reaction, waiting for her to break down.

She'd squeezed his hand. She wasn't certain whether it was to reassure him or herself. And she'd closed her eyes against the white walls, the pale face, and fear that was building.

Beep...Beep...Beep...

She squeezed the hand in hers and forced her tired eyes to open. They protested to the movement. She tried again and managed to open them into slits. The bright fluorescents caused her eyes to float closed in defense. She moaned softly and urged herself to try again.

"Come on, darlin'. Open your eyes."

She wanted to smile but her lips wouldn't move. So, she settled for forcing her eyes to open again.

The fluorescents burned brightly, causing her eyes to water and blur. She wanted nothing more than to let her eyes drift closed but the hand squeezing hers made her keep them open. She blinked rapidly until everything fell into focus.

"'Ata girl."

She followed the sound of the voice, focusing on that noise as too many others pressed for her attention, and found the familiar brown eyes. They were filled with concern but he was trying to hide it. She could tell by the forced smile on his face. He would always try to hide how he truly felt if it would protect her.

"It's nice to see those blue eyes again."

She tried to respond but the words caught in her throat. She tried to swallow and was suddenly aware of the bulkiness of the apparatus in her mouth, down her throat. She felt the panic fill her. She wanted to reach her arms up and yank it out, whatever it was. Her hands were pinned to the bed.

"Darcy!...Darcy!..."

Cooper's voice cut through the panic and her eyes found his again.

"That's there for a reason, darlin'. You can't pull it out." He gave her hands a squeeze, placed the morphine button back in her hand, and sat down with a sigh. His lips fell into a tight line.

She felt the object he'd placed in her hand. Felt the button on top of it. The panic was returning, creeping back up her throat as she became aware of the waves of pain jolting through her. She couldn't isolate it. She couldn't identify where it was coming from. It was everywhere. It was blinding.

The tears welled in her eyes. She felt them roll down her cheeks as her vision blurred. She slammed her thumb down on the button. Her eyes fell closed and she tried not to focus on the pain, tried not to think about the cause of it.

She let herself tumble into darkness.

* * *

Cooper watched the nurse walk away. The monitor had brought her running over. Darcy's heartbeat had risen to a shocking level. It was stable now. She was stable now. But that didn't stop his own heart from racing.

The room was bustling. It was the burn unit, after all. But he'd tuned out the noise of the other patients and families hours ago. Every now and then he would glance around himself a little surprised that there were other people in the room. As far as he was concerned, there was just Darcy. She was all that mattered at the moment.

He ground his teeth together and ran his thumb over the back of her hand. She was asleep again. They told him it was shock, from the pain. They told him that she would wake up again. But he remembered too clearly the panic in her eyes, the fear and the pain. And his heart broke for her.

He was afraid. For the first time in all of their time together he was afraid for her.

First to third degree burns. Two small skin graphs. Not to mention minor physical injuries from the crash itself. It was the worst shape she'd ever been in. It never should have happened.

He was still trying to wrap his head around it. There was going to be an investigation. There always was when something this severe happened. The industry took care of its own. But that didn't change the fact that she was laying there in a hospital bed in too much pain to remain conscious for more than a few moments.

He looked up when the privacy curtain was pulled aside and felt the fist around his heart loosen ever so slightly as the familiar figure stepped forward.

"How's our girl doin'?" Evelyn McKnight's voice was an odd mixture of Irish lilt and southern twang.

Cooper offered his mother a smile, gave Darcy's hand a squeeze, and got to his feet. "She was awake for a moment, but it didn't last long."

"Come here, dear." She waved him over and wrapped her arms around him. He was more than a head and a half taller than her, but it didn't matter. He was still her little boy.

Cooper took a moment to indulge in her familiar scent and the feeling of having her arms around him. He always felt like a child around his mother, it didn't matter how old he was.

He lingered in the embrace for a moment. Trying to block out the sounds of the hospital room around him. With a heavy sigh, he pressed a kiss to her blond, bobbed hair and stepped out of her arms.

"She's going to be okay." He tried to smile but it fell short. "She has to be okay."

Evelyn took her son by the elbows and examined his hands and forearms, which were wrapped carefully in white gauze. "And how are you, lad?"

He scowled down at her. "It's not important, mum. She's all that's important right now."

"To hell it isn't! First and second degree burns you crazy amadán. What on earth were you thinking?"

He looked into her cornflower blue eyes knowing that she was worried about him, knowing that was her job. "I wasn't thinking," he mumbled. The lie tasted bitter on his tongue but he let his eyes drift closed, aiming for sheepishness. His mother had always been able to tell when he was lying.

She sighed and patted his cheek. "How about we get you something to eat and I'll talk sweet nothin's 'bout your sisters."

He glanced over at Darcy who was sleeping peacefully under the influence of the morphine. "But..."

"She'll be fine for an hour, lad." She steered him by his elbow towards the door. "You've got to eat. You've always been too skinny."

Cooper gave a soft smile and let his mother lead him out of the room. There was no arguing with the woman when she got an idea in her head. Not to mention, he really did need to eat.

He cast one last glance at Darcy before they left the room and swallowed the panic that threatened to rise up again. She would be fine for an hour. She would be fine in general. They both would be.

Chapter 2

T*wo Months Later…*

She was in the middle of the ocean. At least it felt like the middle of the ocean if she kept her eyes closed and let her mind wander. And she had no intention of returning to reality at the moment. It held nothing pleasant for her.

She wished she could be out in the ocean with the water surrounding her. She missed the water, missed swimming. But she wasn't allowed to swim yet. She wasn't even allowed to splash around in the bath.

The breeze hit her from across the water and she drew in a deep breath. The action caused pain to radiate across her back and down her arms. She cursed her own stupidity and ground her teeth as she rode out the wave.

"Goddamn it all to hell," she muttered keeping her eyes closed out of spite. "Just Goddamn it."

"I see you're having a cheerful morning."

She slatted her eyes open to glare at Cooper as he sat down beside her on the outcropping. She accepted the coffee gratefully and looked out to see that the sun was well above the horizon now.

"Thank you," she muttered, wrapping her hands around the mug.

"Oh don't thank me," he laughed. "Alice is the one playing nice. I know better than to bother you in the morning."

She continued to glare at him, but there was a smile tugging at her lips. “I'm a perfectly pleasant person.”

“You're a dirty rotten liar.” He sipped his coffee and grinned.

It was easy to be with her now. She'd been chomping at the bit to get out of the hospital. They'd only escaped a week ago, only made it to the house two days ago, but she was a whole different person with her freedom. She was in familiar territory, she had her family around her, and she was on the road to recovery. Or at least that's what he told himself.

Darcy sipped her coffee and shrugged. Then grimaced at the motion. Everything still hurt and the painkillers barely took the edge off. She felt Coop's eyes on her and didn't meet them.

“It's nice to be back here. I haven't been to this house in a few years.” She looked out at the water, at the boats floating in their moorings and the ones already making their way out to deeper water. It was peaceful here. It was exactly what she needed. And that's why he'd brought her there.

“The parents make it up every summer, and Anna comes up with the family a few times a year, if she can swing the vacation days. But it doesn't see nearly as much action as it used to.”

“What about the twins?”

He chuckled. “Bea sneaks up here with her flavour for the month for a weekend away, but for the most part Beth stays away.”

“And Charlie is still playing soccer.” It wasn't a question so much as a statement.

“You know she'll never give that up. They'll have to drag her off the field and make her take a real job.”

“Can you picture it?” She glanced over at him, her eyes glinting with humour. “Charlie tied to some desk?”

"I think she would kill someone or at least end up on the Internet for some violent work outburst." He gave a loud laugh at the image that formed in his mind.

Cooper McKnight was the youngest of the McKnight clan with five older sisters. A fact that, as a kid, had driven him crazy, but as an adult he appreciated more than anything else. His family meant the world to him and, as far as they were all concerned, Darcy was part of the family.

She enjoyed the sound of his laughter, his real laugh. So much of their interactions lately had been forced. She knew that he was trying. She knew that he was worried. But more than anything, she just wanted her friend back.

She glanced back towards the house, making sure to turn her whole torso and not put pressure on her neck. But it hurt nonetheless. "Is Alice expecting us in the house for breakfast or something?"

Coop grinned sheepishly. "Technically that's why I was sent out here in the first place. Something about pancakes and bacon?"

She swatted his arm. "There's bacon fifty yards away and you didn't tell me!"

He jumped to his feet before she could hit him harder. "C'mon then." He offered her a hand and helped her to her feet. She grumbled at the assistance, but he knew she appreciated it.

Darcy had always loved the McKnight's house up in Nova Scotia. The house was situated right on an ocean inlet. It was easily a hundred years old and if a house could look like a gingerbread house, it sure did. The house was three stories of brown siding and red-trimmed windows. The basement walked right out onto the lawn and the main floor was encircled with a covered porch.

Evelyn had her green house and Cooper had a workshop in the old carriage house. It had originally been meant for

Duncan, but the man had never been all that handy, much to his disappointment.

There were six bedrooms and three bathrooms along with the regular living spaces. It was hard to find a place that could hold the entire McKnight clan, but the house always managed to be comfortable without being over-crowded. Darcy was just happy to have more than one bathroom.

They climbed the steps to the porch and walked into the kitchen. It was a cramped space with it's big harvest table, butcher-block countertops and teal cupboards. But it never failed to be welcoming even when there was barely room to move.

The smell of bacon and blueberry muffins hit her immediately. She zoned in on the platter of bacon on the sideboard, next to it was a plate of pancakes and a basket of muffins. A smile tugged at her lips.

"You will make some man very happy one day, Alice," Darcy praised reaching for a muffin.

"Why would she need some random man?" Coop moved to the stove and bent to kiss his oldest sister on the cheek. "She's got me."

"And a lot of help you are, Coop." She shot him a stern glance but there was laughter in her eyes. "I suppose you're not even going to stick around to wash up?"

"Well, you know… I've gotta do that thing… with that stuff…"

Darcy smacked him and rolled her eyes. "You're going to wash the dishes, you idiot, or I'll tell your mum."

His eyes went wide. "You wouldn't."

She grinned as she popped a blueberry from the muffin into her mouth. "Try me."

Alice choked on a laugh as she poured herself a coffee. "She's got you there. Now eat before it gets cold."

Coop shoveled a good portion of the platter of bacon onto his plate followed by five pancakes. He refilled his coffee mug and then settled down at the table. He watched Darcy put a few pieces of bacon on her plate and a single pancake then join them at the table. He doubted she would eat any of it.

The last to sit was his sister, as always. He glanced over at her curiously.

"Speaking of mum, when will she and dad be coming up?"

Alice watched her brother shove bacon into his mouth and shook her head. Some things never changed no matter how much time passed. She ran a hand through her dark brown, bobbed hair and again regretted cutting it so short. It was much easier when she could tie it back.

"Dad said they'd be up before Canada Day. You know he never misses the fireworks. Not to mention the party."

"So any day now, maybe." Coop grabbed a muffin and popped a chunk in his mouth.

"Dad's working on a project."

Coop nodded. That was all the explanation that was really needed. His father was a computer software developer. He'd sold his start-up to Apple twenty years ago and now he just took odd jobs for different companies, not because they needed the money but because he got bored. His projects could last a day or six months. It had always been a little over Coop's head.

Darcy sat quietly and ate, watching the interaction. She had always liked being around the McKnights. She'd always thought they were what a family was supposed to be like: loud, bickering, happy, and welcoming. She'd never had any of those with her family, expect for maybe the loud part. If there was one thing the van Dykes did well it was be loud.

She pushed back the memories of her small childhood apartment, the stink of alcohol, and the dim lights. She didn't want to dwell on that when she was in the warm kitchen, with it's mint green cupboards and butcher block counters. The kitchen that held memories of baking cookies, dancing on Duncan feet, playing cards, and sharing stories. The kitchen that was filled with happiness. She needed to focus on that right now.

She picked absently at the remainder of her muffin and wondered why Alice went to all the trouble. Sure she appreciated it, but she was quite capable of fixing her own breakfast. She wasn't an invalid.

"How are you doing today, Darcy?"

Alice's voice snapped her out of her thoughts and she glanced over to meet the familiar hazel eyes. They were not filled with concern like Cooper's always were; they were assessing and critical.

She shrugged and grimaced at the action. She had to stop doing that. "I'm fine."

Alice rolled her eyes. "Yeah, because everyone believes that lie."

Darcy scowled as Alice got up and rounded the table and tugged off the light sweater she wore. Darcy knew that it was useless to protest and it was painful if she did. She had tried before. It was simpler just to let Alice do her examination and move on.

Alice pulled aside the strap of Darcy's tank top and looked at the skin across her shoulders and down her right arm. The colour pallet ranged from the pink of new skin to the bright red of still healing burns. The minor skin grafts had taken well. There was a small infection early on but the hospital had handled it. And after the risk of future infections had been diminished, the hospital had agreed to release Darcy into Alice's care. As a doctor at Atlanta Medical Centre they had deemed her fully qualified to handle the personal recovery of Darcy.

She scanned the grafted areas. They were redder than the other areas but that was due to healing not because of infection. The rest of the skin looked like it was coming along well. There would be some discolouration, which was to be expected, and some puckering, which couldn't be avoided. But it could have been worse.

"How are the meds working?" Alice asked as she placed the strap back in place and draped the sweater over the back of the chair.

"What meds?" Darcy glanced up at her and heard Coop snort from across the table.

"You're an asshole, Coop. Don't encourage her." Alice kept her eyes level with Darcy. "Is the hydromorphine working?"

Darcy grumbled. "It takes the edge off."

"Are you taking it when you're supposed to?"

Darcy shrugged but stopped halfway through the gesture. "Every now and then."

"Damnit, Darcy!" She slammed a hand down on the table. "If you don't take the fucking meds they won't work."

"Ease off, Alice." Coop was half out of his chair, ready for action.

"No!" She glared at Darcy who was staring at the table. "I'm in charge of her care and she better damn well listen to me. I know you're both stubborn as mules, but this is serious."

"Sorry…" Darcy mumbled. She stared at the remaining food on her plate but what little appetite she'd had was gone.

"Darcy," Alice leaned on the table and drew in a deep breath. The girl worried her. She was just another younger sister as far as Alice was concerned, and just as frustrating as any of her other siblings. But she was concerned about Darcy's behaviour, about her recovery. And it was stressing her out.

"Darcy," she began again. "Take your pills. Use your cream. Do your range of motion exercise. No running. No swimming. No lifting. Sit, relax, and do nothing."

"Yes ma'am." Darcy met Alice's eyes and hoped hers didn't reflect the hostility she was feeling. "Now if ya'll don't mind, I'm going to excuse myself before I piss anyone else off."

"Darcy…" Coop went to follow her but his sister held up a hand to stop him.

"Let her go. She needs to work through some of this on her own. All you do is help her ignore it or remind her of what used to be."

"You're in a mood this morning."

"And I wonder whose fault that is?" She rolled her eyes.

"What? Me?" He stood and started gathering dishes. "I've been nothing but be a wonderful brother. Look, I'm even doing the dishes!"

She scoffed, but sat back and let him work.

Chapter 3

Eight Years Ago…

She curled up in a tighter ball and put her hands over her ears. Perhaps if she pretended she couldn't hear the banging on her door then it would stop and then she could get some sleep.

She knew he couldn't get in. Cooper had assured her that the lock would hold even against her father. But he was yelling and pounding and her faith was faltering ever so slightly. So, she pulled the covers over her head and tried to drown out the noise.

There was no one to stop him tonight. Her mother would be working until 3am down at the pub. There was no one to tell him to calm down. No one to distract him with another beer and some sports reruns. It was just her, alone in her room. Listening to him pound.

He wanted her to come out. He wanted her to have a few drinks with him and watch the game. She'd heard it all before. It didn't matter that she was fourteen and couldn't drink. It didn't matter to him that it was a school night. He just didn't want to be alone.

"You ungrateful little bitch, open the damn door!" He pounded a few more times. "Too good to spend quality time with your dear ol' dad? Think you're better than me?"

"Go away…" she groaned pulling her knees tight to her chest.

She was more tired than angry at this point. She just wanted to sleep. She had a major math test in the morning and she really didn't want to be propping her eyes open with toothpicks.

"You and your mother are exactly the same. Greedy, ungrateful cunts! Never spending any time with me."

"Just fucking go away..." she sighed letting her head fall back against the wall, the covers pooling around her waist.

"I don't need you!"

She heard him give the doorframe a solid smack and stomp off down the hall. A few years ago she would have prayed for one of the neighbours to call the cops. She would have even taken one of them knocking on the door to tell him to keep it down. But the neighbours knew Andy van Dyke well enough to know that it was best to turn their TVs up and ride it out.

That wasn't an option for her. She could call the police, but she didn't want to do that to her father. She could call the McKnights to come get her but it was already well passed 1am and she didn't want to do that to them. She could have crawled out onto the fire escape and hid up on the roof until he passed out, but it was hotter outside than in the house, which was a rare occurrence.

So there she sat, knees to chest and head resting against the wall. She heard the TV blaring in the other room and hoped that he was done for the night, prayed that he was done. She closed her eyes and wished for sleep to come.

* * *

Present Day...

She flopped down on the bed with a groan. Everything hurt. She wasn't going to tell Alice that and she definitely wasn't going to tell Cooper that. She wanted them to think she was on the mend. They were concerned enough as it was without adding to it. And she had never been good at taking other people's concern.

"Argh!" she screamed into the bedspread and rolled over onto her back.

She gritted her teeth and refused to let out a noise. The last thing she needed was for one of them to be walking by the door and hear her scream. She rode out the pain, her eyes closed and her fists clenched at her sides. When she no longer felt like she was going to throw up, she opened her eyes.

She glanced at the pill bottles on her night stand and grumbled. She knew that she should take one. She also knew that she wouldn't. Not now. She'd have to take one before bed in order to sleep. She never made it through the night without one, no matter how strong-willed she was. The best she could do was ride out the pain during the day and hope the drugs did their job at night.

It was late morning. She knew that she shouldn't be exhausted but she could feel her eyes drooping even as the pain levelled out. She knew that she could nap, knew that she was encouraged to nap. But the idea irritated the hell out of her.

She had always been an active person. The idea of lounging around pissed her off to no end. But even if she wanted to try to do something, she knew she couldn't. She was stubborn, but she had always been honest about her limitations. At the moment she could barely take a deep breath without wanting to cry, which meant she definitely couldn't run a mile let alone her standard ten.

The soft tap on her door had her opening her eyes to stare at the ceiling. "If you're waiting for me to tell you to come in, Coop, you're gonna die of old age in that hallway."

She heard the door creak open. It had always creaked. It didn't matter how much Duncan oiled it every year, it had never fixed the problem. She'd accepted it as one of the many quirks of the house and wondered why he kept trying to fix it. But Duncan McKnight had always been a fixer.

She felt the weight drop down on the bed beside her. The smile tugged at her lips unconsciously. "Since when do you knock?"

Coop glanced over at her but her eyes were still closed. "Seemed like the thing to do in order to avoid bodily harm."

She chuckled and turned her head to meet his gaze. "Like I'm prone to violence."

"Only on days that end in y." He reached over and ruffled her hair. His mother had cut it for her just after the accident. Her once butt length hair had been chopped off close to her head. He hadn't seen her hair this short since she'd chopped it off herself when she was eight. Still, he thought it suited her.

"Pfft, hardly." She rolled her eyes. "And it's not my temper you should be worried about. I thought Alice was going to start throwing things."

"She means well." He shrugged as he laid down and folded his arms behind his head. "Anyhow, she's gone to run errands, or escape the house. I can never really tell. But we've got the place to ourselves."

"Do you really think she ran off?" She pushed herself up on her elbows and gritted her teeth against the new pain. "I didn't mean to make her angry. I was just – "

"You were just being you," he cut her off. He glanced up at her and sighed. "You're stubborn. You always have been." He sat up and crossed his long legs. "But on this one you can't be the driver yet. You're not even shotgun. You're stuck in the back seat with the child locks engaged."

"Fuck." She glared at him and struggled to sit up. "I hate it when you're right."

"But I so often am." He grinned and knew she would have hit him if she'd been able to.

"Bullshit."

"Believe what you want." He shrugged and ignored her eye roll. His gaze landed on the pile of medication on the nightstand and his grin fell away. He clenched his jaw and pushed down the wave of emotions that wanted to well up. It wasn't the time or place for him to lose his composure. "Have you put your cream on yet?"

Darcy's lip curled at mention of it. She hated the moisturizer the doctor had prescribed. She knew it was important. And she knew that it was working. But she hated having to put it on. Because it was the one thing that she couldn't do by herself.

"No," she grumbled.

"Well up and at 'em." He moved off of the bed and stood looking at her, hands on his hips. "Don't make me ask twice."

She rolled her eyes. "You're impossible."

"You love it."

He tried to keep the mood light as he helped her out of the light cotton shirt she wore. He knew that any fabric against the burns was painful but he also knew that the only alternative was wearing no clothes at all. So, she wore she lightest, baggiest cottons and dealt with it.

He set the shirt aside and picked up the tub of antibiotic cream. Darcy stood in front of him, her back to him and her arms at her side. She'd never really had much of a sense of modesty, at least not around his family. The problem with growing up around only women is that he'd gotten too accustomed to their various states of dress.

He examined the burns that radiated across her shoulders, down her back, and over her right arm. The areas where the skin had been partially grafted were redder than the rest, despite the fact that they were healing. The first-degree burns on her mid back were starting to peel, and the other second-degree burns were pink and starting to brown in places as they healed. The skin was puckering around the graphs and rippling, but the majority of the burned areas remained smooth underneath the damage.

He gritted his teeth and drew in a deep breath.

"Are you going to just stand there or put on the damn cream?" she snapped and knew she shouldn't. But damn it, she was standing shirtless and she hated every minute of it.

"Sorry," Coop mumbled as he uncapped the tub and gently smeared the cream over her back.

She jerked at the contact but couldn't deny that the cream felt nice. It always took some of the heat out of the burns and made movement easier for a few hours. The only problem was that in order to have the cream applied the burns had to be touched, which hurt as much as the cream helped. She sucked in a breath as his fingers moved close to the grafted area.

"Fuck that hurts." She closed her eyes against the wave of pain that hit her and fought the urge to vomit.

"Sorry!" Coop bit his lip but continued to rub the cream in knowing that it was best just to get it over with.

"Just finish, please," she mumbled digging her fingernails into her hands to try and focus the pain elsewhere.

He smoothed the cream down her right bicep, rubbing it gently over the grafted area, and then capped the tub. He set it on the nightstand and helped her back into her shirt. When she was dressed, he noted that her face was pale and her breathing was heavy.

"Will you take a fucking painkiller for Christ's sake?" Coop ran his hands over his face and groaned in frustration.

She blinked back the tears that threatened to well up. She could taste the bile that had crept up the back of her throat when he'd touched the second graft. If it had been Alice in the room she would have been glib, waited for her to leave, and then thrown up in the trashcan. But she couldn't pull anything on Coop. He knew her too well.

She glanced at the bottle of hydromorphine and felt her stomach roll. She hated those pills. It was her second day at the McKnight's coastal home and she hadn't slept since she got there. The pills had made her drowsy but the nightmares had kept her awake. She didn't want to sleep. Without the stronger meds from the hospital sleep wasn't something that came easily.

Instead she grabbed the bottle of extra strength Tylenol, dumped four into her hand, and gave him a small smile. She took the bottle of water from her nightstand and swallowed the pills. "Are you happy?"

Coop rolled his eyes but decided not to push the matter. He would talk with Alice about it later. Right now he just wanted to distract her from the pain he knew she was in. "No, but I'll take what I can get. You want to wash that down with some ice cream floats?"

"It's not even noon." She glanced at the alarm clock, but realized she'd thrown a towel over it so she couldn't watch the minutes tick by last night.

"Since when have you cared? It's ice cream." He held out a hand. "The boys down at Dave's have been asking about you. I'd rather show them the real thing than keep telling tall tales."

"You mean lies."

"Details." He rolled his eyes. "Are you coming or not?"

She eyed his hand skeptically for a moment, mostly for show, then gave a sigh. "Fine…it's not like I have anything better to do."

Chapter 4

They took Coop's bike down to Dave's place. Given the chance, she avoided being in a car as much as possible. The minute she closed the door her hands started to shake and she felt the panic take over. The bike was different. A different beast entirely. The only moment of panic she had was when she put on the helmet. But then she would wrap her arms around Coop, feel the bike rev to life beneath her, and it would all fade away.

It took only ten minutes to drive from the McKnight home to Dave's place. Coop took his time, letting them both enjoy the drive and the outdoors. They'd been there for barely two days. He was just trying to enjoy being back in his hometown. Even though he'd only spent the first four years of his life there, he had always felt more at home in Chester, Nova Scotia than Senoia, Georgia. And more so, he was just trying to distract Darcy.

Dave's Place was crowded with its usual mid-week brunch crowd. He parked the bike to the side of the narrow building so that he didn't take any prime parking away from the locals. He'd had them jump down his throat one too many times over it that he'd learned his lesson quickly. So, he parked out of the way, waited for Darcy to swing off, and took her helmet.

"It looks the same as it always has." Darcy glanced over at the restaurant with its faded sign and cracked paint. The same cars filled the lot that had been there five years ago, and she was sure the same ones would be there five years from now. Very little changed in Chester, she had always liked that about the town.

"What? Did you expect it to?" Coop shot her a grin as he held the front door open for her. The bell jingled, a friendly sound if it didn't cause every eye in the place to turn towards them.

Darcy watched a grin spread across Dave's face as the old man stood up from the 1950s style diner counter. "What's goin' on?"

She had to laugh. Dave was old as time. He would never tell anyone how old that was exactly, but he still insisted on coming in to work at the diner. She had always admired his persistence.

"Oh ya know, I figured I could find some food here if I looked hard enough." She approached the counter with Coop beside her. "I don't suppose you've got any lyin' around?"

Dave let out a deep-bellied laugh. "Ya always were a smart-mouthed one, Darcy." He waved to the stools at the counter with their cracked leather tops. "Come sit. The young lass will fix ya something."

She watched him wander off as his granddaughter made her way down the counter to them with two menus. "I doubt you need these." She grinned as she handed them over. "But I'll leave them here anyway."

"Two root beer floats, Em. And we'll think about lunch." Coop gave her a wink as he settled down on the stool. He watched Darcy gingerly take a seat, but the look of pain on her face was only momentary.

She had tossed a light jacket on before getting on his bike. He knew that the fabric would be painful for her, but he also knew that she wanted to avoid the looks from the locals. If there was a downfall to a small town it was that nothing remained a secret for long, no matter how private the matter was.

"Still flirting with Em I see." Darcy rolled her eyes as the girl walked away. "You'll break her heart."

"It's harmless. She knows it. Besides, last I heard she was chasing after Ronnie Freeman."

She raised a brow and stifled a laugh. She may not have grown up there but she'd been around enough to know the locals. It didn't take long. "She'll eat him alive."

"Which is why he's running," he chucked.

"Cooper McKnight, as I live and breath!"

Darcy turned to see the two women approaching, both easily in their late seventies, perhaps eighties. "Barely," she muttered, but kept her smile in place as they stopped by their stools.

"Edith and Doris, are you two out terrorizing the local men again. Two gorgeous, young ladies like yourself outta find a good man and settle down." Coop watched them blush and swat away his flattery.

"Oh you devil, you." Doris fluffed her hair and smoothed down her pastel top. "Always were the charmer. Got that from your daddy, ya did. Not that we see him much anymore."

"I'll be sure to tell him ya said so."

"Cooper, dear, my car's been making the darndest noise every time I turn a corner. It's this strange clickin'. Would ya be a dear and take a look at it for me?" Edith gave his hand a pat and offered a sweet smile that was all dentures.

"Is it perhaps your turn signal?" Coop kept his voice level and held back the laughter that threatened to bubble up. He could feel Darcy grinning at his back. He was used to dealing with the Clooney sisters.

"I told ya, Edith!" Doris smacked her arm and rolled her eyes. "It ain't no strange new noise. You've just never noticed it before."

"Would ya rather me not ask and the car explode? Then where would we be?" Edith threw her arms up in exasperation. "You'd have to drive me to cribbage on Wednesday, and quilting on Friday, and Bingo on Sunday. And I know how put off you get when you have to drive me places."

"I'm your sister. It's your job to put me off." Doris chuckled. "Now lets leave these two alone." She steered her sister away. "It was nice seein' ya, Darcy."

"Likewise," Darcy muttered, but they were already gone. Off to sit with Mrs. Clark, who was at least ten years their senior, and have tea like they did every day. "Those two are something else."

"And they're not even the worst," Coop replied as their root beer floats showed up in front of them. He thanked Em and turned his attention back to Darcy. "Tell me you didn't miss this place."

She pretended to consider it for a moment as she looked around the room. The paint on the walls was fresh-ish, probably a few years old and still keeping its brightness. The blue walls were filled with white-framed photos of locals doing various fishing things and pictures of boats.

The black and white tiled floors were scuffed but clean. The booths were well worn in from the bottoms of many patrons and the juke box in the corner still worked as well as the day it had been installed.

Darcy smiled as she took it all in. "It has a certain charm."

"Damn right it does."

She rolled her eyes and tried not to fidget beneath the jacket. That was the problem with going out in public. Unless she wanted to explain what had happened she had to cover up the burns. And she wasn't exactly in a sharing mood lately.

She took a hesitant sip of the float and savoured the flavour. It had been ages since she'd had a good one. It was nice to be back at Dave's Place, nice to be back around the familiar faces. She just wished it were under better circumstances.

"Still the prettiest girl in the room, even without your long hair."

Darcy felt the hand ruffle her hair before she turned to see the weathered face holding a familiar smile. Bill O'Hare slid onto the stool next to her and placed his ball cap on the counter. He ran a hand through his grey, thinning hair and grinned. He was getting close to fifty, though he would never admit it, and his skin was dark and wrinkled from too many days out on the water.

"Well aren't you still charming as ever." She picked up his ball cap and put it on her head. "I like the short hair."

"It looks good on ya, kid. What brings you to my end of the world?" He flagged down Em for a coffee and settled down against the counter.

"Oh just lookin' for a little R&R. The people are nicer up here."

"Now who's the charmer?" He downed half his coffee and glanced at Coop. "And you're keepin' an eye on her? She's a wild one."

"Like I could ever stop her from doin' anything." Coop caught Darcy's eye roll but ignored it.

Bill chuckled. "You come out to the boat sometime and pick up some lobsters for ya mama." He grabbed his cap off Darcy's head and placed it firmly back on his own. "Now I'm off ta see a man about a boat."

She watched him go and shook her head. Bill was an odd man. He never said more than a few words at one time, and half of them made no sense at all. "Lobsters?"

Coop chuckled and pushed his empty glass across the counter. "Don't ask. It's a long story."

"I would figure by now I would know all of your stories." She raised a brow.

"A man is entitled to a little mystery."

"Oh, that's cute." She rolled her eyes and pushed her glass to join his. "McKnight you haven't had a secret from me since I saw you stark naked when you were twelve."

"Fine. Mum barters lobsters for her canned peaches and jam. They trade every summer so that she can have lobster when she goes home for cheap and he gets his fix of peaches. He's got prime catch for the area." Coop shrugged. "They've been doing it for as long as I can remember."

"Is that how ya'll manage to have that lobster cookout every August?"

"Guilty." He grinned. "I'm surprised you haven't asked about this earlier."

"I just figured ya'll could afford lobster." She grinned at his scowl. "Don't look at me like that. You know its true. Now put on a smile. Dave's comin' back over."

They both turned to watch the man approach the other side of the counter. It was difficult to determine how old Dave was. Everyone knew he had great-grand children and had been through at least one war. But beyond that, it was difficult to decipher. Everyone who knew him called him grandpa and he'd been old for as long as Darcy had been visiting the diner.

"You two still here wastin' time?" He swung onto a stool on the other side of the counter and grinned at them.

"Got nothin' better to do on a Tuesday." Darcy shrugged and tried not cringe as her burns rubbed against the material of the jacket.

"Don't ya'll have jobs or some such things?" Dave's brow furrowed as he tried to remember what either of them did for a living. He knew all of his customers, but some days it was harder than others to pull out the details.

"On vacation," Darcy supplied. It wasn't a complete lie.

"You still doing that racing thing?" He grinned as he remembered her job. "The wife and I were watchin' the tube the other day and saw some such thing. I don't understand why anyone does it."

"Mostly for the money." She chuckled and tried not to take offence. People had been questioning her career choice for years.

"Well that's always nice." He turned his attention to Cooper. "And are you still fixing cars?"

Coop gave a nod. "Yes, sir."

"That's a good, honourable profession right there. Me brother used to fix cars. Before the war, that is."

Darcy and Coop exchanged a look but said nothing. They'd heard this one before.

"He died, of course. Left the missus well off and taken care of. But it was still a damn shame." Dave looked thoughtful for a moment then gave his head a shake. "His son became a mechanic, just like his daddy though, so that's something I suppose."

"Well, I like the job well enough." Coop shrugged. It had been a while since he'd gotten his hands greasy. He'd had bigger things to deal with. "Working for this one keeps me busy most of the time."

"Oh yeah, I've got you burnin' the candles at both end. There's no perks to the job at all." Darcy rolled her eyes. "It's not like you get to travel or brush shoulders with important people."

"Bah!" Dave slammed his hand down on the counter for emphasis. No one even turned a head. "That don't matter to a man like this! Simple people we are."

"Yeah, darlin', simple people," Coop agreed sending her a grin and ignoring her glare. "As long as I have grease on my hands and a cold beer I'm more than happy."

"A man of fine taste." Dave gave his shoulder a pat as he got back to his feet. "Now you better feed this one." He wagged his finger at Darcy. "She's wasting away to nothin'."

They watched him wander off and both of them burst out laughing. It took several moments for them to regain composure. Darcy was the first to speak. "God, I wish I knew how old he was. I spend every encounter tryin' to figure it out."

"Right? Every damn time." He shook his head. "I've almost given up, but I'm a little too stubborn for that."

"Don't I know it?"

"Look who's talkin'." He ruffled her hair and took the punch to the arm good-naturedly. "Now, are we gonna eat or are you still full from that muffin you pretended to eat at breakfast."

She looked down sheepishly. She wasn't used to feeling guilty about anything, but she did feel bad about not being a better patient. She really did want to get better. Her body simply didn't want to cooperate in anything that was involved in that process.

"If you order something I promise to eat part of it." She saw his eyes narrow and sensed the beginning of his protest. "That's the best I can do, Coop. Take it or leave it."

"Fine. I'll take what I can get."

Chapter 5

Seven Years Ago...

It was a bad night. Mama had stormed out hours ago to work at the pub and dad had started in on the hard stuff early. She'd been hiding in her room since she'd gotten home from school. Headphones had done little to block out the shouts and the sound of things breaking.

She couldn't blame her dad completely. Her mama was worse when it came to yelling. She always got her two cents in before storming out. Then, in the morning, she would be bright and sunny and always thanking the Lord for all she had.

It was quite a flip side. It was almost as if they didn't realize that she could hear them from down the hall. As if the whole building couldn't hear them go at it.

Everyone in town knew about the van Dykes and their tempers. Everyone assumed that she was just as loud and wild as her parents. She was beginning to wonder why she bothered trying to prove them wrong.

Things had been quiet for an hour now. Her father had either passed out in front of the television again or had finally decided that his anger was being wasted breaking dishes that he would have to replace with his hard-earned money. That revelation usually didn't come until after a few plates but it always sank in eventually.

Whatever the reason, she was grateful. She had homework to finish. And no matter how loud she'd turned up her music she couldn't drown out their voices. Now, in the blissful silence, she could at least hope to start on the algebra she was a week behind on.

If she was being honest, she was behind on all of her homework. She was just waiting for a weekend that she could run away to the McKnight house and plow through all of her over due assignments. At least there she could get some peace and quiet.

She hadn't spent more than 10 minutes on her algebra worksheet when she heard the light tapping on her window.

She debated ignoring it for only half a second. She knew exactly who it was. And when she went to her window there was a smile on her face.

"What the hell, Coop? It's after midnight." She pulled open the window and pulled aside the curtain so that he could fold his 6'0" frame through. Even at sixteen he was tall, but she had a feeling that he wasn't done growing yet.

"I had a feeling you might want to come to my place tonight." He grinned. "And look, you're already ready."

She glanced down at her pajama bottoms and tank top and scowled. "I was doing homework, for your information."

"Well, bring it with ya. Mum is makin' cookies and fully expects me to finish my homework as well." He tucked his hands into the pockets of his Levi's and rocked back on his heels. "I may have told her that I needed your help with algebra."

She scoffed. "Well, aren't you a dirty rotten liar."

"I'm sure she knows it too." He grinned. "Nothin' gets passed mum. But Charlie's up crammin' for her SATs and Bea is home so no one is sleeping."

With a sigh she went to stack her stuff and toss it in her bag. She threw in a change of clothes for school tomorrow and glanced over at him. "You know I was doin' just fine here on my own."

"I'm sure you were." He took her bag and tossed it over his shoulder. "Oh let me rescue you, just once."

"Coop, you're always rescuing me."

* * *

Present Day...

They spent the day doing nothing. Coop had a way of making nothing seem like something, so it didn't feel like a complete waste. They split a clubhouse sandwich at Dave's, which she ate less than a third of, much to Coop's displeasure. They wandered around town for a little bit catching up with the locals. Coop knew everyone despite having spent so little of his life there. But he'd always had a way with people.

By the end of their wanderings he had three cars to work on over the week and a few more that were likely to drift into the house before their vacation was over. Such was the way with small towns. And he wouldn't accept a penny for the work, but they would all pay him somehow. A free meal here, a homemade pie there, or something of the sort. It would all be compensated.

She smiled at the thought. Things worked much the same in Senoia. Her dad had run a rather tight ship when it came to his shop. He'd always demanded payment. But there had still been those customers that couldn't pay. Times were hard. Families were big. But he never turned them away. She'd gotten riding lessons and piano lessons for free. Her mama had gotten quilts and garden vegetables and farm fresh eggs. It was a good system.

It was close to eight before they finally made it back to the house. The activity had taken her mind off of the pain for the most part but as she swung off the bike she felt it settle back in. She discarded the jacket as quickly as she could without injuring herself and hissed out a breath.

Coop cast a glance in her direction, his lips a thin line of worry. "How bad is it?"

She shot him a glare. "Oh wipe that look off your face. I'll live."

"You shouldn't have worn the jacket, darlin'."

"Oh yeah, and spend my first real day of freedom explainin' t'all the locals how I got these." She gave a sarcastic smile. "That would have been loads of fun."

"Darcy..."

"Remind me next time that's exactly what I want to do." The pain was coming in waves now.

"Fine. It was a dumb suggestion. I just don't know what you want." He half lifted his arms in frustration. "I don't know what I can do."

"Nothing." She tossed the jacket over the seat of the bike. "Just give me some time alone, Coop. Before I say something I'll hate myself for later."

She turned on heel and stormed off towards the house. She knew she was being terrible, especially after she'd had such a great day with him. But right now all there was was the pain. She was surprised that she'd ignored it that long, but now it was beating her like a baseball bat to the face. She could feel her lunch rolling in her stomach and threatening to come up.

She raced through the house, ignoring Alice's greeting and whatever words followed it. She took the stairs two at a time and slammed the bathroom door behind her. She barely made it to the toilet before the little she had eaten for lunch came back up.

She drew in a deep breath, squeezing her eyes closed against the pain. And then retched again. She shuddered against the toilet seat and wiped her hand across her mouth.

"Fuck," she moaned.

She waited a moment, unsure if her stomach was done ruining her day. When she was sure she wasn't going to hurl again she got to her feet, flushed the toilet, and washed the puke off her hands. She was in the middle of brushing her teeth when she heard the knock on the door.

"Go the fuck away. I'm fine." She knew she was being harsh but she didn't want to deal with Alice and she definitely didn't want to see Cooper.

She heard whoever was outside test the doorknob, which she'd had enough forethought to lock before tossing her cookies. Then there was a heavy sigh and retreating footsteps.

"Thank God," she mumbled around her mouthful of toothpaste.

She brushed her teeth three times to get rid of the taste of vomit and then finally left her hiding place. The hallway was empty and she made it all the way to her bedroom without witnessing further signs of life. She could hear Coop and Alice talking downstairs, but she didn't follow the voices. She wanted solitude.

She closed her door and locked it. She would have leaned against it and heaved a sigh, as she usually did when she locked herself in her room, but she caught herself before she could. She knew that she'd scream the minute her shoulders touched the wood and she didn't want the attention it would draw.

She did heave a sigh though, gritting her teeth against the pain it caused. She could barely tell one pain from the next right now. Everything was just a wall of pain.

She headed over to her nightstand, noticing the sandwich and bottle of water that Alice must had left there. It made her feel guilty for being rude earlier but she didn't dwell on it. Instead, she grabbed her bottle of pain meds, this time the ones the doctor had prescribed, and shook one out into her hand.

She stared at it for a moment. There was still a large part of her that didn't want to take it. She didn't like what the meds did to her. She didn't like that they made her sleep. If that was what she could call the nightmare-filled darkness they sent her to. But she did like that the pain went away, at least for a little bit.

"Fuck it." She popped the pill into her mouth and swallowed it with the new bottle of water. She was in too much pain to care about the nightmares. They were a problem for later. If she didn't sleep then she wouldn't have to worry about it.

She wandered over to the bookshelf, which held more movies than books currently. Coop had set her up with a television and DVD player the minute they'd gotten there. She hadn't touched it yet, but she had all intentions of making use of it tonight.

She scanned the titles and felt the grin pull at her lips. It was typical Coop to load the shelf with his favourites and completely ignore hers. Not that she hated the movies he liked, far from it. It was more that they were not her 'go to' films when she wanted to waste time. She was more action-adventure and he'd always been big into sci-fi.

She thumbed a few of the cases pondering them until her eyes fell on the *Star Wars* box set. She chuckled and pulled it off the shelf. Well, if she planned to waste the whole night it was best to commit to it. The box set only held episodes four to six, but she knew if she looked hard enough she could find the first three on the shelf.

She remembered when Coop had dragged her to the theatres to see *Episode III*. She smiled at the memory. She'd protested the entire way, but it had been a good movie. She'd never let him know that though.

Deciding she was in the mood for the original trilogy she put episode four in the DVD player. She navigated the start menu then settled down on the bed. She stripped off the shirt she was wearing, careful not to brush it against her burns, and tossed it aside. She debated for half a second how to lie down before grabbing her pillow and flopping down on her stomach.

She didn't get to see whether Hans shot first before her eyes drifted closed and the meds took hold.

Chapter 6

She woke up gasping for air. She clawed at her throat and fought against the blanket she had managed to wrap herself in. She couldn't breathe. The smoke was filling her lungs. All she wanted to do was breathe.

Her eyes flew open and she stared into the blackness. She was trapped. She couldn't breathe. She was never getting out.

She thrashed against the blanket; heedless of the pain it caused, trying to escape, caught between her nightmare and reality. The scream froze in her throat as she noticed the headboard in the dimness of the room.

Her lungs let go and she drew in a deep breath. Drinking in the oxygen as if she would never get another. It was just a dream, her mind screamed at her. Just a nightmare.

She sat up, the blanket now a rumpled mess on the floor bedside her, and took inventory. She didn't remember falling asleep. She'd put on the movie and then woke up feeling like she was suffocating...again.

She rubbed her hands over her face and drew in another deep breath suddenly aware of how much her burns hurt. She wasn't sure what she had rubbed them against while she was thrashing around, likely everything, but they hurt like hell. She cringed as she rolled her shoulders experimentally.

"Well fuck." She closed her eyes and tried to collect herself.

She reached across the bed to the nightstand where she'd tossed a towel over the alarm clock. The LED display told her it was just passed one in the morning. She'd barely managed three hours and she felt more exhausted because of it.

She tossed the towel back over the display and groaned. What the hell was she supposed to do now? She was wide-awake and there was no chance she was going to take another pill. She didn't want to sleep.

She glanced at the sandwich on her nightstand. She was hungry, but she didn't know if her stomach would handle it. She pondered it for a moment before reaching for the bottle of water instead and taking a long drink. She tapped her fingers on her knee and considered her options.

Sitting alone in her room seemed like a sad and lonely idea. So, she did the only thing she could do. She tossed on her shirt, grabbed the box set of DVDs, and went in search of a distraction.

Coop's room had always been in the walk out basement of the coastal home. There were three bedrooms down there, a small kitchenette, and a rec room. It was where all the kids were sent when the adults took over the upstairs. And for the most part, they'd always been fine with it. There was an air-hockey table and a N64. What more could kids ask for?

She took the stairs with as much stealth as she could muster. Alice was currently bunking on the top floor, but she'd get kicked to the basement when the rest of clan showed up. Despite being the oldest she no longer had priority seating in the house. She wasn't one to complain.

Once she got to the basement she followed the nightlight to Cooper's door. He'd plugged it in yesterday saying that if she needed anything to just come find him. Well, she was calling him out on the offer now.

She didn't bother to knock. They'd been friends too long to bother knocking, despite his recent hesitancy. He'd been weird ever since the accident, but she wasn't going to hold it against him. They'd all gone through a lot that day.

"Coop..." she whispered into the darkness. "You awake?" She heard the soft snoring and sighed. "Cooper Joseph Douglas McKnight!"

Coop bolted up in bed, blinking against the darkness, and sputtering. "What? What!"

"I knew that would get you," she laughed moving across the room to click on his bedside light. "Now, move over so I can join."

"What the hell, Darcy!" He blinked at her owlishly against the light then glanced at his bedside clock. "Bloody hell, it's one thirty in the morning."

"And your point? You told me that I could come to you any time I needed to." She sat down on the edge of the bed. "Now, move the hell over." She moved across the comforter. "God you take up so much space!"

He grumbled as he shifted in the bed, still trying to wake up. "Sorry for enjoying my bed," he muttered. "What the hell has you so social? You were in a shit mood when you ran off."

She shot him a glare. "If you don't want my company I'll leave you alone."

She went to move away but he laid a hand on hers. "Darcy, don't be like that. What happened?"

She thought about telling him. She'd come downstairs for company, but she wasn't sure she was ready to tell anyone what happened when she closed her eyes. Not even her closest friend. She was pretty sure he knew. He'd spent almost every night of the two months of her hospital stay sleeping in a chair next to her. But that didn't mean she was ready to talk about it.

"Well you see, I started watching *Star Wars* and realized it just wasn't the same without your sparklin' commentary."

Coop examined her fake smile, wanted to press further, but knew that it would just piss her off. "I thought you hated *Star Wars*."

"Hate is such a strong word." She sent him a sideways glance. "Plus, it's not like you left any movies I actually liked on that shelf."

He smiled sheepishly. "You need to expand your interests."

"Fuck off." She rolled her eyes and tossed the box set at him. "Now, put it on and make some popcorn."

"You want popcorn and a movie?"

"Well, they sort of go together." She shrugged before she remembered it would hurt. "Don't tell me you don't want some."

He scoffed, "Of course I do…now. The power of suggestion is a wonderful thing." He slid off the bed and headed towards the door. "Anything else you want while I'm up and about, darlin'?"

"If your mum still hides cookies down here you should grab those too."

Coop sighed and wandered out of the room. The small kitchenette in the basement had been one of his favourite things about this house. He liked the convenience of not having to go upstairs to sneak food and risk waking up the household. Not that his mother didn't know that he ate the stuff she stocked downstairs. She just preferred that his snacking habits didn't interrupt her sleeping.

Leaving the room smelling like popcorn, he returned to his bedroom with the cookie tin and bowl of popcorn in hand. Darcy was still sitting on his bed, the start menu for the movie playing, and her eyes wandering.

"I see you resisted the urge to start without me."

She chuckled. "It was such a trial to do so." She didn't bother to tell him that she'd already started it earlier. "Now, pass me the popcorn and press play."

"You're so needy."

"You love it." She took the popcorn he handed her and tossed a few pieces in her mouth. She hadn't been hungry at lunch but now she was starving. She supposed it had something to do with throwing up her lunch, but she didn't want to dwell on it.

The popcorn didn't last them long and the cookies were set aside before they could finish the tin. Darcy peppered him with questions as the movie progressed, and he answered them in a good-natured manner, as always. When the credits for *A New Hope* finally rolled, he turned to face her.

"Alright, I'm not putting on the next one till you're straight with me."

She met his serious expression, his dark brown eyes not holding their usual puppy dog playfulness, but she didn't respond.

"Are we becoming insomniacs? Because, if so, I am going to have to plan some daytime naps in order to make this work. Or is this a one-time thing and I can expect to have my bed to myself tomorrow night? I just need to know what I'm working with here."

She sighed. She hadn't wanted to get into this tonight. She was hoping that he would let her be until at least tomorrow. But she should have known better. Cooper was persistent.

"It's not going to be a one-time thing," she muttered running her hands over her face. "At least, I doubt it will be. So you may want to prep for those daytime naps."

"Nightmares?"

Her eyes met his quickly. "How did you guess?"

"You weren't the only one there that day, darlin'." He glanced down at his hands. The burns had healed a while ago, but he could still see where they'd been. "It still comes back to me when I close my eyes."

"How do you sleep?" She drew in a deep breath to calm herself as her heart began to race at the memory of her nightmare.

"Mostly because I have to." He shrugged. "That doesn't mean I don't wake up in a panic. I either manage to get back to sleep or I don't. Coffee and energy drinks go a long way."

"We should buy stocks in them, because we'll be consuming a lot." She took his hands and stared down at the burns that hadn't quite faded to white. "I never thanked you…"

He shook his head. "You don't have to."

He let the serious moment wash over them before ruffling her hair and getting to his feet. "Well, I suppose I'll put in the next one if we're going to be awake."

"Oh, I can't wait." She rubbed her hands together enthusiastically.

"Don't sass. I can just as easily put on infomercials like every other respectable person at this hour does." He wiggled the remote. "I'm gonna keep this on hand just in case."

"You're an asshole," she said it with a smile.

"You say this like it's new information." He set up the next movie and crawled back into bed. Without even bothering to ask, Darcy curled up on his chest. He noticed that the position allowed all pressure to be taken off her burned arm and back so he didn't bother to sass her about it. Instead, he just tried to make her comfortable.

"Now, if I'm going to stay awake for this, so are you. I don't want you falling asleep before we can finish *Episode VI*," he warned and ignored her eye roll.

She was asleep before Luke could meet Yoda. He was glad that she could at least get a few more hours.

Chapter 7

He left her in his room in the morning. She'd slept since just after three. Other than a few whimpers, she'd stayed down at least until six. He was glad for that even if it had meant that he'd stayed awake. The combination of movie noise and another person had been enough to keep her settled. He knew it was a short-term solution, but he would take it for now.

He'd barely dozed off when she'd started to scream. She'd struggled against him and pounded on his chest. It had taken him several minutes to calm her down and he knew that he'd have bruises by the end of the day. She'd finally woken up disoriented, crying, and gasping for breath. Once he was certain she was fine, he'd left her to dig into the cookie tin. She'd said she was going to shower and meet him in the kitchen later.

As far as mornings went his was off to a shit start. When he walked into the kitchen and found his sister already at the table he figured it wasn't going to get any better.

"Morning," he mumbled going straight to the coffee pot and filling a mug. He drained half of it and then topped it back up.

"That kind of morning I see." Alice raised a brow as he joined her at the table, one of her blueberry muffins in hand. "I suppose you have Darcy to thank for that."

He peeled the top off the muffin and took a bite. "She's not taking her meds and she's not sleeping."

"Well, that explains why you look like you crawled out from underneath a rock." She sipped her coffee and took in his tussled hair and sleep-shadowed eyes.

"Thanks, sis. I know I can always count on you for a compliment." He rolled his eyes and started working on the bottom of the muffin. The caffeine was starting to settle in his system but he knew he'd need a few more cups to get through the day. "We need to do something about this."

She regarded him across the table. Her brother had always cared about Darcy. She'd known it the first time the two of them had come to the house when they were in primary school. She'd been in her teens at the time but it was clear to her that they had a friendship most people don't find. She knew that she'd never found it. And the worry he wore on his face, right alongside the sleeplessness, was evidence of how much he cared.

"And what exactly do you suggest?" She set her mug down and spread her hands in surrender. "I can't make her take the pills."

He shrugged as he took his time replying, finishing his muffin and coffee. He knew what he was about to suggest and he knew that she wasn't going to like it. She rarely liked his ideas, but this was pushing it.

"Well, I figured she didn't have to know she was taking them."

"Cooper..."

He caught her warning tone but pressed on. "She's never going to take them on her own. She's in more pain than she'll ever admit to you. Every time she moves it hurts. And she seems to think that taking a few Tylenol will fix things. She won't get better if she keeps hurting herself."

"Don't you think I know that?" She said exasperated. "I'm a fucking doctor. I've seen this a million times. But you can't just give people drugs without their consent."

"She's not exactly in the best place to make personal decisions." He ran a hand through his hair and sighed. "Just mix them in with her yogurt or something."

She raised a brow and took a sip of her coffee. "Oh yes, because that would go over just swimmingly. What if she decides to drink when she doesn't know she's taking the meds? What if she takes them because she actually comes to her senses and she already has a dose in her system? I signed paperwork, Coop. Legal documents. I could lose my license. I'm a fucking doctor!" She set her coffee down more in exasperation than anger. "We don't just randomly drug people."

He watched her expression closely. He knew that she wasn't saying no. He'd spent enough time around her to know when she was telling him that he was off his rocker. He leaned back in his chair and crossed his arms. "You can't, but I can."

She gave a half smile into her coffee. "Now, that's a completely different matter." Her eyes met his across the table. "You're not as slow as you used to be, little brother."

* * *

Darcy locked the bathroom door for the second time in twenty-four hours. She'd never been one to care. Modesty wasn't exactly her strong suit. She'd grown up mostly around Cooper's sisters who'd spent a great deal of time in a state of undress searching for clothes to wear over the years. She supposed that was the benefit of siblings. A person to share things with.

She wanted to lean back against the locked door. She wanted to slide down it and bury her face against her knees. But she knew that the life long habit of hers would cause more pain than satisfaction at the moment. And, at the moment, her body was just throbbing rather than screaming. She wanted to keep it that way for a few moments at least.

She felt bad for ruining Coop's morning. She knew that she should have just stayed in her room and dealt with it herself, but damnit she didn't want to. She was sick of dealing with it alone. Her whole life she'd dealt with it alone, and Coop had been her only shoulder. So, she didn't regret leaning on him last night.

She did hope that she hadn't hurt him too badly. She couldn't help but smile a bit at the thought. He'd rub that one in a bit, and milk it for all it was worth. She was kind of looking forward to it.

She sent a dark glance at the shower and sighed. "So my evil mistress, we meet again."

She hated showering. She'd wanted nothing more than to soak in a hot bath since the accident, but she still wasn't allowed to submerge herself that long. As a swimmer, that irritated her to no end. She wanted to be in the water.

She started the shower at a luke warm temperature. Not too hot or too cold, she was not allowed extremes in life at the moment. She wasn't allowed anything at the moment.

She tested the water with a grumble and then began to strip off her clothes.

She told herself she wasn't going to look. She told herself every time she was in a bathroom that she wasn't going to look in the mirror and see how bad it was. She didn't need to know. The pain was enough suffering, she didn't need the image.

It didn't matter how many times she told herself, she always looked. She always peeked into the mirror and took stock of the damage. This was the first time she'd gotten to see it without bandages and without someone with her telling her 'it's not so bad'. This was the first time she could make an honest assessment.

She stood in front of the full-length mirror and examined the body she used to be so familiar with. It was amazing how quickly a person's body could become foreign to them. She used to be toned, a body comprised of muscle. Now, she was skin and bones. A month and a half in a bed, with limited movement, had taken years of work and destroyed them.

Not that she was particularly vain. She'd never been fixated on her weight or size. But she was an athlete. She always had been. And she felt like the wind could blow over the girl she saw in the mirror.

She ran her hands through her short, bright red hair. She liked it better short. She always had, but her mother had hated it. So, she'd worn it long her whole life after that first mishap when she was eight. It was much easier to manage especially with her limited range of motion right now. She'd been grateful when Evelyn had suggested cutting it off.

She looked tired. That wasn't surprising. The shadows under her eyes stood out against her pale skin making the green of her eyes more prominent. She hadn't been eating and she could tell from her face that she'd lost weight. She wanted to blame the hospital food, but she knew that she'd simply had no appetite. She was starting to seriously miss food.

Finally, she drew her attention to the parts she was really concerned about. She ran a hand tentatively over the spot on her left thigh where the skin had been removed for her grafts. A perfect rectangle. It had scabbed over at first and been so itchy she'd wanted to scream. Now the scab was still there but the pain elsewhere distracted her from the itching. And she knew that the new skin would be coming in underneath it. It would be nearly healed now.

"Well, shorts will never be the same," she muttered as she ran her hand over it again. She'd always have that scar. The weird shaped spot that would draw questions from bolder people and stares from the curious. But she knew that it was nothing compared to where the grafts had gone.

She turned so she could examine her back and right arm in the mirror. She sucked in a breath at the sight and bit her bottom lip. She could make out the two grafted areas. Their grid work design not completely healed into regular skin yet. The rest of her skin was a colour splash of red, pink, and brown.

She knew it would eventually settle into pink and the white of scar tissue. She knew that some of the puckered skin would never lay flat again. She knew that the smoothness of her left shoulder would never be felt on her right again. But just because she knew it didn't mean she was ready to see it and accept it.

She choked on the tears that welled up in her throat and fell down her face. She didn't want this. She didn't want to look in the mirror and remember this every day.

"Why, God damnit?!" She sobbed and yanked at her hair.

If it had been her mirror she would have broken it. Instead, she took a step back and sucked in a breath. She pushed back the tears and rubbed at her eyes.

"Well, this fucking sucks." She sent one last glance at her reflection and, on a whim, flipped it off.

She wasn't the girl in the mirror. She reminded herself as she stepped into the shower, cursing as the water hit her shoulders. She would not be the sad girl in the mirror. She was better than that.

Chapter 8

E*ight Years Ago…*

Darcy let her bike fall to the ground as she jumped off of it. She was surprised that she had beaten Coop to the field. Part of her thought he'd let her win, but when she saw him come speeding up behind her and tumble off his bike huffing she knew that she'd won fair and square.

She grinned at him and picked her bike back up. "I lost you there passed Benson's Farm, what happened?"

He lifted his elbows, which were now skinned, the blood mixing with dirt. "I hit the loose gravel on that turn." He shrugged. "It'll dry up in a bit."

She rolled her eyes. "I'm sure we can find some liquor to clean those off with and a napkin or two." She glanced over at the field, which was crowded with people and pick-up trucks. The barn was alight and the music was blaring. "Do you know any of these people?"

He did a cursory glance and spotted his sister in the distance. "Well Bea's here, so there's that. Otherwise, I haven't got a clue. I'm sure there are a few people we know from school or town."

Darcy's eyes landed on Bea and the cute brunette she had in tow. The smile pulled at her lips. "I think she'll be occupied for the next while, Coop. We'll have to navigate this ourselves."

"Occupied?" Coop's eyebrows drew together in confusion as he glanced towards his sister again, just in time to watch her slip behind the barn with another girl. "What do you mean?"

She looked over at him. They stood at eye level right now, but she had a feeling that would only last another year. She had towered above him last year and it was shocking how much he'd grown in a single summer. She knew she would soon be looking up at him.

"You don't know, do you?" She watched his eyes fill with more confusion and sighed. "Your sister isn't going behind the barn to gossip with Becca."

"Of course she is. What else would she be –" He paused, clamped his mouth shut, and then his eyes widened in realization. "You don't mean…?"

She grinned and reached over to pat his shoulder. "Yup. Bea's snuck back there for seven minutes in heaven with Becca." She tried not to laugh at his gapping expression. "Close your mouth, ya look like a damn fish outta water."

He snapped his mouth closed. "Fine, okay, ya this is fine. But how the hell do you know?"

She shrugged. "Maybe I just know your sister better than you do. Or maybe I was behind the barn with her a few weeks ago." She nodded in the direction of the barn.

Coop sucked in a breath. "My sister or Becca!?"

"I don't kiss and tell." Darcy grinned and sauntered away from him. "Now are you coming to the party or ya gonna stand there lookin' confused all night?"

He ran to catch up but stood silently at her side as they approached the crowd of people. Darcy reached into a cooler and pulled out two sodas, not even bothering to wonder whom they belonged to. She popped the top on her own and offered the other to Coop.

He glared at it and her in unison. "I'm not takin' it till you give me a straight answer."

She debated making a joke there, but decided against it. She really did hate when he was mad at her. "Fine. I didn't kiss your sister." She pushed the soda into his hand. "Happy now?"

"No," he grumbled taking a drink. "What the heck am I supposed to do with this information?"

"You mean the information that effects your life not in the slightest?" She sent him a sideways glance.

"She's my sister."

"So, be happy for her and support her. And if she is unhappy then go beat someone up. That's your job as brother." She shrugged. "And if you think your mother doesn't know about this, you're wrong. She knows everythin'. It's a bit frightenin'."

"And what about you?" Coop scratched his head and averted his eyes.

She felt the heat rise a bit in her cheeks. She wasn't used to feeling embarrassed around Coop. Then again, this was new territory for them. "'Don't ask, don't tell' seems to be the best policy for this matter."

He sighed and took another drink. "And does mum know?"

Now she grinned, because she couldn't help it. "She knows everythin'. It's like ya weren't listenin'." She watched him swallow and wondered what secrets he thought he was keeping from his mother. "Now c'mon, it'll be a boring first year at school if we don't make some friends tonight."

She grabbed his free hand and dragged him towards the crowd of people hanging out by a tailgate.

"Wait, you need more friends than me?"

She sent him a slanted look. "Definitely."

* * *

Present Day...

She came down the stairs and heard the familiar voices coming from the kitchen. She'd figured they would both be there, waiting for her to emerge so that they could assess the damage. She figured she wouldn't keep them waiting.

She carried her tub of cream with her. She knew that after her shower she would need to put it on, so she figured she'd talk Coop into doing it after she forced something that resembled breakfast into her. She could smell the coffee as she entered the room and was glad to see that the pot was still half full on the counter.

Her whole body was tingling from the shower. It wasn't a terrible feeling, but it also wasn't wonderful. It was as though every nerve ending had been awakened by the water and was just waiting to be assaulted. She could barely stand the light tank top she wore and her cotton shorts were brushing against the spot on her thigh.

She tuned out the individual sensations and instead focused on the simple task of pouring herself a mug of coffee. She ignored the stares at her back as Coop and Alice pretended to maintain a conversation. She had to give them credit. They were trying.

Finally, with her mug full and in hand, she turned to face her crowd. "Good morning."

Alice gave her a raised brow look. "Is it a good morning?"

Darcy made a show of glancing out the window and scanning the sky over the inlet. "I dunno, looks a little bit like rain. But it could pan out to be a not half crap day."

Coop chuckled and ignored the glare from his sister. Alice wasn't seeing the humour in it. "Well aren't we cheeky this morning. How's the pain?"

Darcy shrugged and, as usual, regretted the motion. As her skin dried it got tighter and even the slightest movement hurt. "No worse than usual. I'll make Coop put my cream on after I eat."

"Oh will ya now?" He crossed his arms and tried to look insulted.

"As if you have a choice in the matter." Alice rolled her eyes but moved around the table to examine Darcy's burns. They were nice and red this morning, no doubt the result of the shower. She'd warned her against setting the shower head to anything other than its softest setting, but the girl was stubborn. She looked over the grafted areas, checking for tears and any chances of future infections. Everything seemed fine. Despite the hell Darcy put herself through, she hadn't managed to destroy herself yet.

"Well looks like you're all in one piece." She stepped back and went to retrieve her coffee. "At least for now."

"Glad I pass." Darcy smirked, but it was half hearted. "Now, what's for breakfast, or are we back to fending for ourselves?"

Coop nodded towards the fridge. "I made you yogurt with fresh fruit." He watched her curl her lip at that. "What? It's good for you."

"Bacon and eggs is good for me. The verdict is still out on yogurt." She stuck her head in the fridge nonetheless and pulled out the bowl.

"Don't act like you don't like it."

She eyed the bowl of blueberries and strawberries in vanilla yogurt. It did look rather appealing. She had to give him that. "It doesn't look terrible."

"If you don't want it..." he reached for the bowl but she jerked it away possessively.

"I didn't say that." She took a big spoonful and shoved it in her mouth. "Mmmmm, delicious," she mumbled around the mouthful.

"Good." Coop raised his coffee mug to his lips to hide the grin that was forming there. Only Alice noticed.

"Well, I'll leave you two to your mischief." She sent a warning glance at Cooper. "Don't do anything stupid."

"But – " he began to protest but she plowed on.

"And put Darcy's cream on." She put her coffee cup in the sink and looked from one to the other. "I'm off to get our sisters from the airport."

"Which sisters?" Coop inquired and Darcy snickered. It was a legitimate question.

"Beth and Bea are flying in today, from completely different places, of course." She rolled her eyes. "So, I'll be at the airport all day waitin' for them 'cause they're too cheap to rent a car and mum would have my head if I made them."

"Better you than me," Coop muttered.

"Oh, but you get to stay with this ray of sunshine." Alice smiled.

Darcy sent her a glare. "I'm fucking cheerful."

Alice laughed but didn't reply. Instead, she just grabbed her jacket and headed out the door. Darcy could have sworn she was muttering, "I love my job" as she left.

"What the fuck was that about?" She turned to Coop who was grinning.

He shrugged. "I won't begin to try and understand any of my sisters." He reached over and took the empty bowl from her hands. "How was the yogurt?"

She glanced at the bowl. She hadn't realized that she'd eaten it all. "I stand by my original assessment."

"You're impossible." He moved to the sink to wash the bowl and the other morning dishes.

"As if you'd have me any other way."

He rolled his eyes. When he turned around she was handing him the tub of cream. "I suppose we should get this out of the way," he muttered and watched her nod.

They repeated their routine from the day before. She stripped off her shirt and he methodically applied the cream trying his best to ignore how much pain touching her skin was causing her. When he capped the tub of cream she let out a shaky breath and reached for her shirt.

"I can never figure out what is worse," she began as she pulled the shirt on. "The sharp pain like a thousand needles being shoved under my skin or the constant throb that is so persistent you almost get used to it."

He frowned clenching his hands at his side and remembering his own pain, which he knew was nowhere close to what she was feeling. "They both seem to suck."

"No, the worst is the one that hits you in the face, like a baseball bat hitting a home run," she continued as if he hadn't spoken. "Yeah, that one is the worst."

"Is that what happened yesterday?" He regarded her closely, remembering how pale she'd gotten when they'd returned to the house and how she'd run off.

"Hmmmm?" She snapped out of her thoughts and glanced over at him. She could see the concern in his puppy-dog brown eyes. She hated seeing it there. "Yeah, that's what happened yesterday."

She watched him frown deeper and ground her teeth together. "Now, can we stop talking about my miserable situation? You still owe me five more *Star Wars* movies."

Coop forced his mouth into a grin and topped off her coffee mug. "It would only be four if you hadn't fallen asleep during our marathon. Remind me never to pull all-nighters with you again. You're bad at them."

"Am not!" She shouted after him, but he was already running downstairs to grab the movies.

She glared in the direction that he had headed but could feel the smile pull at her lips. It was turning into a good morning. Breakfast, coffee, a movie marathon, and, to top it all off, the dull throb in her shoulders was subsiding. She let the smile spread across her face. It would be a good day.

Chapter 9

Alice sat at the airport and tapped her fingers on her knee. She'd been there for two hours already and her patience was beginning to wear thin. Beth's flight had been delayed, something about a rain storm, but on the bright side it put her landing at almost the same time as Bea, who was coming from somewhere in Europe. She could never keep track of the two of them. The phone calls and emails came through, but they were free spirits.

She'd never been like that. She'd always been the grounded one. The oldest, responsible for the safety of the five younger ones. Not that she hadn't wanted to shake that title a few times. She'd partied when she was younger. She'd had her fun. And then she had committed to college, med school, and her residency. Now, she was finally a doctor. She finally had a hospital to call home. And she was not going to be jealous of her little sisters.

She picked up the paperback that she'd been attempting to read for the last two hours. She'd thought if she could at least lose herself in a book she could make the time pass a little quicker. But she'd never been much of a casual reader. Textbooks had ruined that for her. She read medical journals and case reports before she went to bed now, with crime shows on to fill the emptiness. And she was okay with that.

She closed the book, having not read a word and shoved it back in her bag. There had to be something better to do with her time.

She sighed and scanned the people milling about. Most were waiting for passengers to get off flights, but some stood with their luggage waiting for rides, hoping they hadn't been forgotten.

She eyed the young man across from her standing awkwardly, leaning against his luggage. He put all of his weight on his left leg. She followed the line of his right leg down to the air cast that poked out from beneath his track pants. She eyed his tan.

"I bet you tripped and twisted your ankle," she muttered, glancing beside her to ensure no one was within earshot. "And now you're going to tell some elaborate story about how it happened."

She watched his face light up as a couple entered the room. He made a grand show of hobbling over to them. And in response to their concerned expression exclaimed, "You won't believe what happened!?"

Alice chuckled to herself. She'd forgotten how entertaining it was to people watch. She scanned the people around her and tapped her thigh thoughtfully. There were four pregnant women, at least one she guessed didn't know it yet by the way she was chugging back her Americano. Alice hoped she figured it out soon and laid off the caffeine.

Otherwise, there was just the usual. A few elderly people with hands starting to curl from arthritis. There was a middle-aged man who'd had a hip surgery recently, she recognized the gait and the way he leaned on his cane. But beyond a few cases of the sniffles, she quickly found the crowd around her to be as boring as her book.

Just when she was about to make another attempt at reading she saw the flood of people come in. Leading the pack were two faces she could pick out of a crowd any day.

"Alice!" Beth yelled, waving enthusiastically as she dragged her luggage along. Bethany 'Beth' McKnight was a shorter woman at 5'4", but she still had two inches on Alice and her mass of brown hair was pilled haphazardly atop her head. Beside her, Beatrice 'Bea' McKnight walked empty handed matching her twin in height but little else. They shared a similar slim build, although Bea had always edged more towards boney much to their mother's displeasure. And her hair, partially shaved, showed brown at the roots on her left side, but cascaded in a waterfall of blues and greens on the other side.

Alice looked at the grinning faces with a mixture of happiness and dread. All hopes of a quiet vacation were completely gone now. But still she returned their smiles.

"Bea, where the hell are your bags?"

Bea glanced at her sister and then at her twin. "No hi or hello? We really need to work on your manners, Alice." She rolled her eyes and glanced back towards the doorway as two young men dragged paint-splattered bags in their direction. "Ah, there they are!"

Alice sighed. "Are you leading on strangers again?"

"Did she ever stop?" Beth glanced at her older sister with a questioning expression as Bea went to thank the gentlemen for bringing her bags out.

"Did you pack enough stuff?" Alice wandered over to the three canvas bags and her brow furrowed in confusion. "I thought you were just staying a few days."

"Oh, you know me," Bea shrugged, refusing to make eye contact. "I need to be prepared."

"What she means by that is she's broken up with – insert name – and she's now picking a new country to call home," Beth sighed. "Really Bea, you should make them move next time."

Bea shrugged sheepishly. "Well, the lease was up on my flat, and I was getting sick of Barcelona. I mean, how much Italian architecture can a person take in during one lifetime?"

Alice and Beth exchanged a glance but didn't push. The whole story would come out eventually after a few drinks and some down time. Right now they all wanted to get out of the airport. Alice bent to pick up one of the bags and grunted at the effort.

"Christ, what do you have in here? A dead body?"

"Don't say that too loudly, they might check," Beth laughed but gave the bag an experimental tug and stumbled. "Damn it, Bea. What are you hiding in here?"

"Just art supplies. I had to clear out the flat before I left. Anything I could safely fly with came with me. Everything else is going to be sent on to Senoia in a week or two. Shipping cost me a fortune."

Alice drew in a deep breath and prayed for calm. She usually needed it when dealing with her sisters. "Well, either get one of those trollies or find another set of young men, because we're not getting these to the car on our own."

"So, now you want me to flirt." Bea rolled her eyes.

"Only if you want this to come home with us."

Alice watched her walk off and knew it wouldn't take her long to find a willing gentleman to help carry the bags. It never did.

"I have no clue how she does it," Beth sighed following her twin with her eyes as she crossed the room. "She's always been able to."

"She did get all the social skills," Alice teased. "That's why you work with animals."

"Fuck off!" Beth punched her lightly in the shoulder but couldn't completely argue the statement. Animals were a lot better company, most of the time. She found them less judgmental.

It took them an hour to get out of the airport for no reason other than Bea took twenty minutes thanking the gentlemen who carried her bags and exchanging numbers that she would never follow up on. They weren't her type. But she still smiled and flirted and sent them on their way.

Once everyone was in the car, that Alice had parked in the closest lot possible without getting ticketed, they heaved a collective sigh. Beth sat shotgun and Bea stretched out across the back seat already looking half asleep. Alice smiled as she started the car. It was good to have her sisters home. Even if there were still two to come.

"So, how is the patient doing?" Bea inquired from the backseat.

Beth watched Alice bang her head gently on the steering wheel. "You really shouldn't do that."

"I'm not driving yet," she grumbled. But sat back up and ran both hands over her face. "Darcy is Darcy. Stubborn as always."

Bea grinned. "I always liked that about her."

"You would," Alice muttered. "It makes her a terrible patient."

"But she's going to be fine?" Beth's voice carried the concern that was written plainly on her face.

Alice shrugged. "The worst part of it is over, medically at least. The danger of infection and such. The rest she has to deal with, and that might actually be worse for her than spending weeks in a hospital bed."

Alice put the car in gear and pulled out of the lot. Neither of her sisters commented on that, both aware that Darcy had a battle ahead of her. They didn't know the extent of it, she knew. No one but her parents and herself had seen Darcy since the accident. She hadn't wanted any of them at the hospital. So, this was her welcome home party. Alice just hoped it didn't end poorly.

* * *

The world was black and dark. Her eyelids felt like they were glued closed and she struggled to open them. She could feel the blanket laid over her, feel the weight of it. Everything felt heavy.

She tried to stretch and ground her teeth against the pain that shot through her body. Everything was sore. Not just the burnt areas. It was as though every muscle in her body was protesting against the very idea of movement.

She put her effort into stretching her legs out. She wasn't sure how long she'd been lying there. All she could remember was watching *Star Wars* and then nothing. Just blackness. Now she was curled up on the couch, under a blanket, and the room was silent.

She tried to keep her eyes open as she straightened out her legs and struggled into a sitting position. She rubbed at her eyes and tried to get rid of the heavy feeling there. It felt as though she had slept for days but a glance at the wall clock told her it had only been a few hours. Still, it was the first solid sleep she'd had in a while.

She scanned the living room. The TV was turned off. Everything was cleaned up. The only sign that anyone had been in there was her blanket on the couch.

She pursed her lips. Coop had obviously been worried. He only ever cleaned when he was worried. Otherwise, he was one of the messiest people she'd ever met, besides herself. She preferred to think of hers as organized chaos.

She took a moment to wonder if she could trust her legs before she pushed herself to her feet. She was doing her best to ignore the pain that was rushing over her in waves. She ground her teeth together and dug her nails into her palms. Eventually, the waves subsided and she felt the nausea pass. When she knew she was steady on her feet again she headed towards the kitchen where she hoped she would find Coop, and potentially coffee.

He was exactly where she thought he would be. His feet propped up on the chair across from him, a coffee mug on the table, and a western novel open on his lap. He'd given up reading it to stare out the kitchen window at the bay. The coming and going boats holding his interest for the moment.

It was rare that she saw him like this. He was so often a ball of energy, always needing to do something with his hands. Always needing to fix something. But when they were here, in the one place he had always felt most at home; she found that he truly relaxed. It was the only time she ever saw him pick up the western novels she knew he was fond of and the only time she ever saw his mind wander.

"Wondering what it would be like to be a fisherman again?" She watched him jolt out of his thoughts and glance over at her. The relief that was clear on her face perplexed her. "What's got that look on your face?"

He shrugged, irritated that he couldn't mask his emotions better. "You were just asleep for a long time. I was starting to get worried."

"Are you ever not worried, Coop? I think you need a new hobby." She chuckled and headed towards the coffee pot. "How old is this?"

He glanced at his own cup, which had gone cold long ago. "You'd better make a fresh pot."

"Well, you're useful," she sighed but dumped the contents nonetheless and set to work on the new pot.

"I can get that for you, darlin'." He moved to get up but the glare she shot him stopped him dead.

"I'm not a fucking invalid, Cooper McKnight. I can make a pot of coffee." She watched him sit back down, slowly. "And stop it with that darlin' shit. What happened to calling me Red or Sparky?"

He adverted his eyes and mumbled under his breath.

"I'm not glass. I'm not gonna shatter if someone makes reference to what happened." She slammed the lid on the coffee maker and pressed the start button. "I may kill the next person who tries to coddle me though."

Coop ran both hands over his face and back through his hair. "You're fuckin' impossible, Darcy. You know that right?"

"You love me anyway." She flashed a grin and crossed to pick up his mug. "Now, how about I fix ya a fresh cup and we chat before your sisters get back."

"Why don't ya just kill me now."

"Awe, that would be too easy," she laughed and set to work.

Chapter 10

Darcy put her mug in the dry tray as the car pulled into the drive. She heard the doors slam and felt the smile tug at her lips. She'd been having a good time chatting with Coop, bothering him about anything that came to mind. She'd always been good at bothering him. And he took it with all the good grace that he usually did, which was none.

She could hear them coming up the front porch steps and cast a knowing glance towards Coop. "Last chance to run away."

He glanced towards the door at the end of the hallway and sighed. "I've been dealing with them a lot longer than you have. You sure you don't want to run?"

"And miss this?" She hopped up on the counter and grimaced at the pain that shot up her arm at the motion. "Never."

The door swung open and she watched Alice walk through, followed by Beth, and a vibrant Bea carrying a brown paper bag. Alice opened her mouth to speak as they made their way down the hall but Bea cut her off.

"We brought cake!" She held up the brown bag triumphantly. Smiling winningly, she moved to set it on the counter as she entered the kitchen.

"Cake?" Coop glanced from Bea to Alice, brows raised.

"Well, I couldn't really think of a better way to say 'Glad you're not dead and welcome home!'," Bea explained giving

Darcy a sideways glance. "Susan at the bakery was very confused when I asked her to write that on the cake."

"Bea!" Coop's voice held a warning tone.

"Did she?" Darcy lifted the edge of the brown bag to peer inside sharing none of Cooper's offence to the statement.

"Nah, we settled on 'Welcome Back' as a happy compromise." Bea glanced at her brother. "Pull the stick out of your ass, Coop. Darcy likes the cake."

He crossed his arms and grumbled but didn't say anything else. Alice sent him a sympathetic glance and joined him at the table. "You had to know you weren't gonna win."

"I didn't have to know anything," he grumbled.

Darcy jumped down from the counter and gave Bea a light hug. "Thanks for the cake." She glanced over at Beth. "And hello to you too."

Beth gave her a gentle hug and glanced down at the burns. "How are you doing?"

Darcy shrugged and ground her teeth against the pain that shot across her shoulders. She really needed to stop doing that. "I'm alright. Can't really complain."

"I'm sure you can, but you won't." Beth smiled and gave her hand a squeeze. She glanced around the kitchen and sighed. "It's good to be back here."

"In comparison to…" Coop paused. "Where the hell were you again?"

Beth rolled her eyes and pulled up a chair at the table. "North Carolina, where I've been for the last five years. So glad you pay attention."

"Oh don't get mad at him." Bea slid into the chair beside her twin. "His attention is often focused elsewhere." She sent Darcy a glance.

"Oh, don't look at me like that. I'm hardly a distraction. He manages to be forgetful all on his own." Darcy grinned as Coop sunk deeper into his chair. She always felt a little bad for him when his sisters were around. Even though this was only half the clan he always became the target being the only boy. So, she did her best to divert the focus when she could.

"What about you, Bea? Where have you been hiding?" Darcy leaned against the counter and regarded the twins. They were so similar in so many ways and yet so different.

"Oh here and there." Bea grinned at the collective eye roll from around the table. "Fine, I was in Barcelona."

"Weren't you in Rome before Christmas?" Darcy crossed her arms because her sweatpants lacked pockets. She made a mental note to steal a pair of Cooper's later.

"Well yes, but there was a bit of a mix-up with my patron there and I figured Barcelona might be a better fit." She ran a hand through her hair and twisted up atop her head, similar to her sisters. "Now I'm looking for a new fit...again."

"What happened in Barcelona?" Coop sat up in his chair. He had always enjoyed his sister's escapades.

"Well, there was this man named Marco who didn't take too kindly to how fond his wife Penelope was of me." She shrugged as Alice sighed. "What? It's not like I did anything."

"You never do. These things just happen." Beth gave Bea's shoulder a pat but didn't bother to hide the grin on her face. "But what was the deal with your flat mate?"

"Oh, now that's a whole different story. I definitely did something there."

"I don't want to hear about it!" Coop shot up from the table as if he'd been bitten. "Who wants cake?"

"What?" Bea looked at him, all innocence. "It's nothing you haven't heard before, you prude."

"Exactly, I've heard it before." He shook his head as if trying to clear a mental image. "I didn't want to hear it then.

Don't want to hear it now. If ya'll are gonna have those talks I'm leavin'."

"Awe, don't be like that," Darcy laughed and sent Bea a glance. "You owe me an explanation later. But for now we'll play nice." She moved towards the brown bag. "Let's have a look at this cake you brought."

"It was my idea, just so ya know," Bea announced as she got up from the table to join Darcy at the counter.

"And my money," Alice countered. "So, if you want all the credit, you owe me a twenty."

"It was a group effort." Bea sent Alice a smile and glanced at Beth. "Beth even helped."

"I did very little," she mumbled.

Darcy gave them all a smile. "Well, I appreciate it nonetheless. And stop being modest, Beth. I'm sure you kept these two from killin' each other the whole ride home. That's greatly appreciated."

"And very difficult," Coop added and flinched at the glares he received. If he ever forgot his place they were quick to put him back in it.

"Cooper, make coffee and I'll cut this cake." Alice instructed pulling the cake out the bag.

"Darcy just made a pot not too long ago – " he began but stopped at the look she gave him. "Fine, fine. I'll make the damn coffee."

"Herbal tea for me, please," Beth called over. "Mum probably still has some in the cupboard."

"Are you still on that healthy livin' kick, sis?" Coop looked at her skeptically. She had always been slim and he's never heard her talk negatively about her weight before. So when she'd announced her veganism and organic living lifestyle a few years back they had all been caught a little off guard.

"Oh, don't look at me like that." Beth rolled her eyes and moved towards the cupboard to get the tea herself. Then muttered a curse when she saw it was on the top shelf.

"I'll get it." Coop grabbed it. "And I'll make it for you. I was just curious."

"If you saw what I saw at work you wouldn't eat meat ever again either. As for the other stuff, well I don't exactly have the healthiest habits so I take them where I can get them."

"And that means this tea that smells like it tastes like crap?" Coop sniffed the box and pulled a face.

"It's not so bad," Beth laughed.

"Not all of us can live off of cheeseburgers and good intentions," Bea said as she shoved a forkful of cake into her mouth.

"And what exactly are you living off of?" He gave her a once over. She'd always been the slimmer of the two, edging towards too thin. But he knew that she ate her fair share when she wanted to.

"Oh you know, vodka and sugar. What else is there really?" Bea chuckled and moved back to sit at the table.

"Oh, only five real food groups that everyone else lives by." Alice handed Darcy a piece of cake. "Please tell me you have higher standards than this lot?"

"I, at least, don't pick my tomato off my cheeseburgers, but sadly my standards aren't that high." She grinned at her cake.

"Tomatoes are evil, " Coop protested.

"Here-here!" Bea cheered in agreement, raising her fork in the air.

"Sometimes I wonder how I'm related to any of you," Alice muttered.

"You don't have to wonder with me," Darcy grinned. She took her coffee from Coop and moved back to the table. "The cake is great, by the way. Susan make it?"

"One can assume so," Beth shrugged. "I still wonder if she employs elves in the back. How else does she have time to make everything and raise three children?"

"Clearly it's magic," Bea agreed. "This cake tastes magical."

"That's only because it's the only real food – and I use that term generously here – that you've had since leaving Barcelona. And who knows what you were eating there." Alice joined them at the table. "Mum is gonna freak when she sees you."

"I'll wear my baggy shirts, like always." Bea shrugged, her eyes downcast. She didn't like to make her mum worry, but her appearance was a work-in-progress.

"Ya, cause that always works." Beth glanced at the cake longingly but pushed her piece away. Someone would eat it. "We both get the same lecture every holiday. She means well."

"Course she means well." Alice ran her hands through her short hair. She envied her sisters their ability to tie theirs back. "She loves us. And she's proud of us. But she's still mum."

"Ain't that the truth," Coop muttered.

"When are they gracing us with their presence?" Beth looked at Alice for an answer.

"Likely tomorrow, since Friday's the holiday. And they aren't gonna travel on the holiday. That would be ridiculous." Alice emphasized the last word and imitated their mum's voice.

"Ah yes, ridiculous," Darcy chuckled.

"And Anna is coming up with the family on the holiday because she could only land the Friday evening and the Saturday off work. And Charlie will get here eventually." Alice shrugged. "Like every holiday, it all works out. Everyone will show up in time for the show to start. "

Bea grabbed the piece of cake that Beth had abandoned. "Well, I'm not saving them any cake."

Darcy laughed and felt at home, like she always did with the McKnight clan. "I don't think they would expect any different."

Chapter 11

S*ix Years Ago...*

She locked the apartment door and leaned against it for a moment. She was supposed to be in her room. She was supposed to be in bed. Tomorrow was a school day and she needed sleep. But her father was drinking, and she knew that he would start yelling shortly.

She'd been getting good at figuring out when he would start. Some nights were better than others. Sometimes he just passed out in his chair with the race on. Some nights he was silent. But there were nights when he barged through the door too amped to sit in his chair. Those nights she had started leaving. She didn't trust the lock on her door to hold him back any longer. So, she just left all together.

It took her a few minutes to get down to the street. It was just passed eleven. Hardly late, but the streets of Senoia rolled up pretty early. Except for the crowds at the pub downstairs and the restaurant down the road, there was very little in the way of activity. A few kids would still be out, teenagers without curfews or with parents who didn't care. But no one would notice her.

What she didn't expect to find when she hit the street was Cooper parked at the curb, helmet under his arm, leaning against his motorcycle. She eyed the Honda Rebel that he'd spent the last six months working to fix. It had been in quite the state of disrepair when he'd purchased it and now it looked brand new.

"When'd you finish it?" She crossed her arms and leaned against the building. She didn't want to approach him or the bike. She wasn't sure if she could handle either at the moment. She's just wanted to go for a walk. Clear her head until her father passed out for the night. She hadn't been ready to deal with Cooper at the moment.

"Today." Coop grinned down at the bike and ran a hand lovingly over the seat. "Your dad helped me put the final touches on it in between jobs."

She gave a tight smile. "Well congratulations, Coop. She looks great."

He glanced up from the bike and met her gaze in the dim of the streetlights. He'd caught the tightness in her voice, the attempt at happiness. He read the sadness in her expression and pushed off from the bike.

"He's drunk again, isn't he?" He glanced up towards the apartment but didn't need to see her nod to know he'd guessed right. "Did he hurt you?"

Darcy went to respond but Coop was already kicking the lamppost in frustration. "Motherfucker! I told him to lay off today. He'd already drank half a case of beer before I went home for dinner." He raked his hands through his hair. "I swear to God if he laid a hand on you."

"Simmer down, Coop. The neighbours'll hear." Darcy glanced down the street. People were used to her father's yells by now, but if anyone caught wind of her and Coop's conversation there would be a great deal more interest in the goings-on of the van Dyke household.

"I don't give a fuck about the neighbours." Yet Coop still crossed towards her and lowered his voice. "Did he hurt you?"

She met his gaze and held it for a moment. "He didn't lay a hand on me." She searched his expression, begging him to calm down. "He didn't get a chance. I left soon after he came home."

He placed a hand gently on her shoulder. "Good," he sighed trying to bring his temper back down. "Good call."

"I thought so." She smiled weakly.

"I'll never understand how a man can be so decent most of the time and be a complete ass once he gets into the liquor." Coop shook his head.

"Mama always said it was the curse of the drink." Darcy shrugged. She had always believed her mama made too many excuses for her dad. But she also knew that when he was sober he was a decent, loving man. And she enjoyed those days when they came about.

Coop sighed. "She would say that."

Darcy shrugged, trying to brush off the conversation as much as the memories of less lucky nights. "So, are we just going to stand here or are you going to show me what you've spent half a year doing?"

He paused for a moment, not wanting to ignore the fact that she was clearly trying to ignore what was going on, but still eager to show off the bike. He finally settled on the bike. He knew there would be plenty of chances to talk about her father later. "Well, c'mon. I'll take ya for a ride."

She rolled her eyes. "I thought you'd never ask."

* * *

Present Day…

Darcy pulled her shirt back on and cringed at the motion. She'd convinced Coop to put another round of cream on her burns so they were both hiding in his room. Although it wasn't much of a hiding place. No sooner had she pulled the shirt on when Bea come through the door.

"I figured you'd be in here." She smiled and flopped down on the bed.

Coop sent her an offended look but she ignored it. "You have your own room ya know."

Bea rolled her eyes. "But Darcy is in yours right now." She patted the mattress beside her. "C'mon, I owe you a story."

"Seriously?" Coop threw his hands up in frustration as Darcy joined his sister on the bed. "Why my room? Of all the places in the damn house."

Ignoring him Bea turned to Darcy and grinned. "So, I was invited to this threesome just after I got to Barcelona…"

"That's it!" Coop covered his ears and headed towards the door. "I'm out of here. Christ, you two are ridiculous."

Darcy laughed as the door closed behind him. "It's a little sad that it still works."

"Every time," Bea chuckled but the smile on her face fell away. "But really, Darcy, I did come to chat with you." She watched the other girl's eyes drop to the mattress. "Now we can talk about my sexual exploits overseas if that's what you really want, or you can fill me in on what's really going on here."

Darcy sighed. She'd always been able to talk to Bea. It didn't matter about what. When she'd been confused about her sexual preferences, she'd come to Bea. When she'd crashed her car and couldn't tell Coop, she'd come to Bea. She trusted no one else in the world as much. Coop had been her friend for ages, but Bea knew her darkest secrets.

"I promise you, your sexual exploits are much more interesting," Darcy countered picking at the bedspread.

"You don't know that." Bea shrugged. "They could be full of old people and saggy bits. You don't know what happened over there." She laughed as Darcy cringed. "C'mon, D, tell me how you've really been."

Darcy ran a hand through her short hair and wondered where the hell to start. "I'm terrible. That's not what anyone wants to hear, but that's the truth. Everyone wants me to be on the mend, to be getting better. But it's shit. It's all so fucked up."

"I don't care what everyone wants." Bea pulled her legs up to sit cross-legged on the mattress. She leaned forward. "I just care what is going on with you."

Darcy sighed. "I don't sleep. Every time I close my eyes I'm there again. I can't eat. I don't know if it's the pain or the meds, but half of what I put in my mouth I throw up. And the pain. Don't even get me started on the pain."

Bea closed her eyes for a moment to stop the tears that threatened to well up. She couldn't lose it now. She needed to keep it together. "Have you been taking your meds?"

Darcy glanced down at the mattress again, avoiding Bea's green-blue eyes. "No."

"Darcy..." Her tone wasn't angry but exasperated and a little confused.

Darcy met her gaze. "I don't want to take them. I don't like that they make everything go away. It's too simple. It's not right. It's too easy. Too much like downing a bottle and forgetting."

"Oh honey, it's not the same as your father." Bea laid a hand over Darcy's and gave it a squeeze. "You need these. Just for now. This isn't a forever thing. But if you don't take them it's never going to get better."

Darcy blinked at the tears in her eyes and ignored the ones that were already falling down her cheeks. She knew that Bea was right. She knew that she should take them. But the thought of it terrified her. "What if they make me like him? What if I can't stop taking them once I've started?"

Bea considered it for a moment. They weren't simple questions. They weren't things to be taken lightly. "You've got all of us to help you. Don't forget that. We're all here with you on this. You're never alone." She grinned. "Even if you really want to be."

Darcy smiled and wiped at the tears. "I'm glad you're here, Bea. Even if it's just for a short while."

"Who said anything about a short while?" Bea caught her surprised look. "Oh, you're not gettin' rid of me that easily. I've got no where better to go."

"Does Mum know yet?" Darcy raised a brow.

"Nope, nor do the others. But they'll catch on soon enough." She grinned mischievously.

"Oh and I'm sure Coop will take it well."

"He loves me." Bea waved it off as if it wasn't an issue. "Besides, we stay out of each other's way."

"You are in his room," Darcy pointed out.

"Whose side are you on?"

She raised her hands in surrender. "Switzerland here, but only when it comes to you two."

Bea ruffled her hair. "Now if you don't mind, show me the damage so I'm not shocked by it in front of everyone else."

Darcy turned so that all of the burns across her back and down her right arm were visible. The only bit covered was by the strap of her tank top. She heard Bea inhale a breath and let it out slowly.

"I had noticed your arm when we were eating cake, but that's worse than I thought."

"Well, you certainly know how to make a girl feel better," Darcy joked and managed to make Bea look sheepish.

"Sorry, I didn't mean to say you look bad or anything. It just looks like it hurts." She glanced at it again and let out a heavy sigh. “Promise me you’ll take your meds, D. I need you to promise.”

Darcy met her gaze and nodded. “I promise, Bea. I’ll do my best.”

She nodded, knowing that was really all she could expect out of the girl. “And you’ll talk to me about this? I know you have Cooper, but he’s well, Cooper. You’ll let me know what’s really going on.”

“Promise.” Darcy held out a hand, pinky raised.

“Well, that’s just too cheesy to pass up.” Bea linked pinkies with her and shook. “I suppose we should let Cooper know he can have his fortress of solitude back.”

“Or you can tell me about your sexual exploits and we can keep him in exile for a while longer.” Darcy grinned.

“I like the way you think.”

Chapter 12

She couldn't breathe. She couldn't see. The visor of her helmet was plastered with mud and she couldn't reach to wipe it clear. Her chest felt tight as the harness held her in place. She choked on the smoke. So much smoke.

She tugged at the harness trying to find the release but it wouldn't budge. She felt the panic clawing at her throat as she struggled to draw in a breath. She needed to get out. She needed to see.

She tried to reach for her helmet again, managing to wipe some of the dirt away. Through the corner of the visor she saw it. The flames licking up the side of the car. She registered the heat that went with the smoke clogging her lungs.

Her panic doubled.

She didn't know which way she was. Right side up? Upside down? She just remembered sliding off the track. The rest was blackness. Now there was just the need to get out, to get free. The need to escape the flames before they got any closer.

She pulled on the harness straps. She fought with the release but it wouldn't let go. It was getting harder to breathe. The heat was getting unbearable. She didn't want to look back over at the flames to see where they were. She didn't want to think about it.

When the scream registered to her ears she didn't believe it was coming from her body. But mere seconds after the scream she felt the pain. And then there was only darkness.

Darcy shot up in bed, the scream still echoing in her ears. Her heart racing and her hands shaking, she ran them over her face and through her hair. It took her several moments to realize she wasn't in her own bed.

She glanced over at Coop who was sitting up in bed, his back propped up against the headboard and the western novel discarded on the nightstand. His brown eyes were alert and focused on her.

"Shit Coop, I'm sorry –" she began rubbing a hand over her mouth and trying to calm herself down.

"Don't start with that crap." He gave her a warning look. "I knew what I was getting into when I said you could sleep here again."

She leaned back gently against the sheets, careful to put the weight on her left side. "That doesn't mean I don't feel like an ass for waking you, and probably the rest of the house."

Coop shrugged. "They'll get over it." He glanced at the ceiling above him. "Besides that, the twins can sleep through anything and Alice knows you're in here tonight. No one is leaving their bed."

"And you get the joy of not sleeping?" She sent a meaningful glance towards the novel.

"Sleep is overrated." He grinned. "And I've been meaning to read that for a while now. No time like the present."

"You're an asshole," she muttered as she curled up against him and rested her head on his stomach. She took solace in his steady and calm breathing.

He wanted to run a hand over her hair but resisted the urge. Certain gestures just seemed too intimate. Instead, he laced his fingers behind his head and leaned back against the headboard. "Care to share with the class what had you screaming?"

She glanced up at him, meeting his slanted gaze. "As if I need to explain."

He shrugged. "I just wanted to know if it was the same film role going tonight or if we'd switched things up. For all I knew, aliens could have been invading and wiping everyone's memories in that dreamland of yours."

"I think I would have preferred that," she muttered against his shirt.

"Awe now, don't say that. Havin' no memory of me would be tragic." He could feel her grin but still took the fist to his thigh good-naturedly.

"You're so self-centred." She shifted trying to get more comfortable. "I don't think forgetting you would be that bad."

"It would be tragic, darlin'." He accepted her glare at the nickname, but he was becoming quite fond of it. "On a different note, you slept a few hours. Did you take your meds?"

She pulled a face, curling her nose at the statement. "I took some Tylenol," she admitted with a yawn. "I promised Bea I would start taking the meds, but I looked at them last night and I just couldn't. I'll try in the morning."

He sighed and knew that she likely wouldn't take them in the morning either. He wasn't above sneaking them into her food again, but he didn't want to make a habit of it. "Well, let me know if you are successful in that."

She murmured an agreement against his shirt, but she was already drifting back to sleep. Coop shifted down so that his head was at least on the pillow and hers on his chest then turned off the bedside light. He'd give them both a chance to sleep. He just hoped that they could manage it.

* * *

Coop left her sleeping in his bed early that morning. He'd managed to catch a few hours but he knew that he wouldn't get any more. He was too wired at the moment.

She'd woken up twice more, screaming from whatever dreams were plaguing her. He had a pretty good idea what she was seeing. He saw similar things when he closed his eyes, but he knew it was worse for her. There was no room to compare.

He'd talked her into taking one of her pills after the last episode. She'd been on the verge of tears from the pain and the nightmare had her shaking. He knew that, even if they weren't a perfect solution, they would allow her to sleep for a little while. They would make her numb for a few hours.

He wasn't as lucky at the moment. He couldn't close his eyes without seeing her, trapped and struggling. He couldn't close his eyes without hearing her screams. It didn't help that half the time the screams were real. Every time she woke up screaming, he was back there at the raceway. Every time she woke up screaming, his heart stopped for a moment and he had to remind himself that it was just a dream. He had to remind himself that they were both safe.

He closed the door softly and hoped she would sleep for a few more hours. He knew that she needed it. The drug-induced nap she'd taken yesterday wasn't nearly enough to catch her up.

It was just passed six in the morning and the sun was pouring through the patio doors. He debated walking down to the water to watch the sun finish its assent. He could swing by the garage and see if Dr. Dillon had dropped off his truck like he was supposed to.

The sound of footsteps above him stopped him before he could move towards the patio door. His brow creased in confusion. With the exception of Alice, there was no one else in the family that would be up this early, and Alice was likely sleeping off her late night like the twins.

He took the stairs two at a time, all thoughts of his outside adventure gone. He rounded the corner into the kitchen and skidded to a halt, his bare feet catching on the laminate flooring.

"If you didn't run in the house you wouldn't 'ave that problem," Evelyn McKnight announced from her place at the table, cup of tea in front of her. She smiled at her son's shocked expression and tossed her bobbed hair out of her face. "Mornin'. Bet ya weren't expectin' us till later."

"Mum!" Coop crossed the room and scooped her up into a big hug that had her laughing. He swung her in a circle and then sat her back down in her chair.

"Now, don't be showing off. Then she'll expect that sort of hello from everyone."

Coop glance over at his father who was at the stove laying bacon in a pan. He grinned. They shared height but little else. Whereas Coop was lean muscle, his father had the composition one would expect of a software developer. His glasses dangled from the front pocket of his shirt and his dark hair was a tussled mess. And Coop knew that the beard he was sporting was more a result of lack of caring over the last few weeks than actually trying.

"Da!" He circled the table and wrapped his father in a warm embrace. "What are you doing here so early?"

Duncan McKnight shrugged and glanced at his wife. "Well, Evie thought it would be best to catch an early flight, which really meant leavin' last night."

Coop looked from one parent to the other. "Are you sayin' you got in last night?"

"Now, now, no need to fuss. We got in and went straight to bed. It must have been well after two in the morning." Evie looked at Duncan for confirmation.

He nodded. "Oh yes, well after. The whole house was quiet."

"You didn't hear anything then?"

Evie looked genuinely baffled. "I don't know what you're referring to, boyo. The house was quiet as a church when we got here."

Coop looked at his mother, searching her face for any sign that she had heard Darcy's screams last night.

She met his stare straight on and didn't waver. "Are you gonna tell us what you're so concerned about or is it best left be?"

Coop sighed. "It's nothing." He caught the look his mother sent his father. "Don't be like that. It's really nothing to worry about."

He knew it was hardly worth lying to them, but he didn't feel like explaining at the moment. Nor did he feel like it was his place. If Darcy wanted to explain things to them that was her decision. He would only take so many liberties when it came to her personal life. There were boundaries.

Duncan, sensing the tension building in the room, cleared his throat as he placed some cooked bacon on a plate. "Why don't you be helpful and get started on the potatoes."

Coop gave him a grateful smile as he went to retrieve the potatoes from the bin.

"And the coffee's fresh, if you want some," Duncan added.

He cast a glance at his wife who sat at the table with a knowing look on her face. She sipped her tea and met his gaze over the mug. Yes, they would have to talk about it later, he knew. But some things were best left until after the sun was up and everyone had caffeine in their systems. Some things were best approached delicately. It wasn't exactly the McKnight way, but they were learning to make exceptions. And for Darcy they would always do that.

He looked over at his son, pouring coffee with his shoulders still tense. He hid it well, but there was no real way to hide it from them. Yes, they would talk about it later, he thought as he went back to the bacon. But for now they would have breakfast and be a family. For now that would be enough.

Chapter 13

Fourteen Years Ago...

Darcy sat in front of the old TV with its bunny ears and bad colour. She knew it was old because Coop had a new TV. But it really didn't matter as long as she could watch Bugs Bunny.

She didn't know where her parents had gone. They'd left a while ago, but they usually left her at home with the TV when they had things to do. She was good and she didn't get into anything. She just sat and watched the TV until they got home. If she was good then maybe she would get a treat. That was what Daddy had said when he'd left. She liked Daddy's treats.

She laughed at the TV. Wile E. Coyote would never catch the Road Runner. That was just how it was. But he just kept trying.

She heard the keys in the apartment door and smiled. They were home. She would sit there until they saw her. She would show them that she'd been good first. Then she would see if they had gotten her a treat. Maybe mama had gone to the bakery and gotten Miss May's butter tarts or a nice cobbler for desert.

She heard the door close and counted down from ten. She always gave them ten seconds to put down whatever they were carrying. Then she got to say hello and help unpack things. That was her job.

5...4...3...

She heard the movement behind her, still several feet away. Coats were off. Things were set down. Shoes were almost off.

2...1...Go!

Darcy got to her feet and ran towards the door. She heard her mama say something but the words didn't reach her ears. She wrapped her arms around her Daddy's waist, happy to see that her head reached his belly now. He'd just said the other day how tall she was getting.

"Daddy!" she announced. The words flew out of her mouth as he grabbed her long hair in his big hand and yanked her away from him.

"Daddy?" she muttered, looking at him with eyes filled with tears from the pain of having her hair pulled and neck yanked back.

He curled his lip back in disgust and pushed her to the side, ignoring the fact that she fell firmly against the kitchen cupboards before hitting the floor.

"Andy, calm down."

Darcy heard her mama use her angry voice but she couldn't process anything beyond the pain in her head and on her cheek. "Daddy," she mumbled against the tears that streamed down her face.

What had she done wrong? She'd been good. She'd watched TV like she was supposed to. Why was he so angry?

"What do I want with that brat? I wanted a son, damnit, Liv! I wanted a boy. And all you give me is that scrawny brat that you dress up like a little doll." She heard him spit the words out like they were something that tasted bad. "She'll never be what I wanted."

"Don't say that."

"Just get her out of my sight. I can't stand the sight of her now."

Darcy heard her Daddy storm off towards the living room as she tried to push to her feet. She couldn't see passed the tears that streamed down her face, but she knew her way to her room well enough. She heard her mama say something from behind her, but she closed the door anyway and put her chair up against it.

So he didn't want her to look like a girl, she thought looking at her reflection in the mirror attached to the back of her door. Fine. She grabbed the craft scissors from her desk and started cutting.

* * *

Olivia van Dyke had never seen her husband so mad, not without the drink in him. She'd known Andy since high school. She'd known his temper when she'd married him, but she'd also known that he was a good man under it all. She'd never imagined he would do this.

Her hands shook as she handed him a beer, the one he'd requested, and then left him to his football game. He'd be good for the evening, she knew. He had enough beer in the fridge to get him through, and he would calm down by tomorrow. Perhaps tomorrow he'd realize what he'd done, what he'd said.

She wiped her mouth with the back of her hand, a nervous tick she'd developed over the years, and headed down the hall to Darcy's room. Now that he was handled she needed to make sure her baby was all right. She knew it should have been her first priority, but she also understood his temper too well to ignore him when he had a good mad on.

Olivia pushed open the bedroom door – Darcy hadn't secured the chair nearly as well as she'd thought – and saw her daughter sitting on the bedroom floor, craft scissors in hand, and red locks in thick pieces around her.

"Oh Lord," Liv whispered wiping her hand over her mouth again before hurrying into the room. She ran a hand over her daughter's shockingly short hair. She blinked back the tears that welled up in her eyes as she took in the bruise that was blossoming on her cheek and her blotchy, tear-stained face. "Oh honey."

"He said he wanted a boy," Darcy mumbled against the tears that threatened to fall again. She brought her gaze level with her mama's. "I thought maybe if I looked more like a boy he might want me more. Do you think he'll still want me?"

Liv's heart broke for the little girl sitting in the pile of her own hair fighting for her father's love, even as her anger built towards the man who was tuned into the TV in the other room. The man who had caused this. She ran a hand over her daughter's hair again and made herself smile.

"Of course he'll want you, darlin'. He's just havin' a bad night. Tomorrow it'll all be better."

She pulled her in for a hug. She was still so small, Liv thought, yet tall for her age. She pressed a kiss lightly to the bruise forming on her cheek and then tugged her to her feet.

"Come now, darlin'. We're gonna go see Miss McKnight tonight. See if she can't fix this hair of yours." She gave her hair a tussle. "Grab your pjs."

He didn't even notice them leave, but Liv had known that he wouldn't. He was comfortably settled into his chair now and focused on the game in front of him. She wouldn't let herself think about how much that irritated her. She had to focus on getting Darcy out of the house, getting her taken care of.

She buckled Darcy into the back seat and pressed a kiss to the top of her head. It took ten minutes to get to her best friend's house. She knew that it was late. Somehow it was already close to eight, but she also knew that Evie wouldn't turn her away. Evie would help.

Liv parked in the drive of the big house and was grateful to see it lit up. She had stopped being jealous of her friend having this house almost as soon as she'd gotten it. It had been a sore spot between them for half a second and then Liv had learned to take refuge in those walls. She had learned how nice it was to have her friend back home and with a home to visit.

She felt the familiar calm pass over her; something she hadn't felt since she'd left the hospital earlier that day. She retrieved Darcy from the backseat and headed towards the front door. With Darcy's hand gripped firmly in hers, she knocked three times.

The porch light came on above her and she heard the dog bark from within, both a warning and welcoming sound. And then her childhood friend filled the doorway.

Evelyn McKnight took in the sight before her. Liv's face was pale against her red hair and her hands shook despite the fact that she gripped her daughter's like it was a lifeline. And then there was Darcy. The little girl's face was blotchy from crying but that didn't hide the bruise blossoming on her cheek, along her jawbone. Her long red hair, that Liv had been so happy about, was now cut about two or three inches from her scalp.

Evie pursed her lips and met her friend's pleading gaze. There was a story here, but it was not something that was told in doorways in the dark. She'd been raised better than that. "Well, c'mon in. I'll put the kettle on."

She stepped back from the door and let them into the house. Her gaze moved down to Darcy and she put a smile on her face. "I didn't know you wanted to be a hairdresser, little one. If you've got a yen to cut hair, I'll show you a thing or two before you get started."

Darcy smiled sheepishly and touched her choppy hair. "I didn't do a very good job."

"It's alright, deary. We'll get it fixed for ya." She ruffled the little girl's hair. "Now, if you want, Coop's still in the livin' room playing on that game box ya'll like so much."

Darcy looked at her mother, eyes bright for the first time in hours. "Can I mama?"

"Run along." Liv watched her go and turned back to meet her friend's intent gaze. "She'll be alright, won't she?"

Evie pursed her lips again, considering. "Kids are resilient." She gave a nod, as if to affirm her own statement. "Now you come along. You owe me a story before we fix that little one's hair."

Evie took her friend's hand and pulled her towards the kitchen, away from the children who were already happily playing in the living room. "Now start talkin' while I get this tea fixed."

"I don't even know where to start, Evie." Liv ran her hand over her mouth and drew in a deep breath.

"I've always found that the beginning's as good a place as any."

Chapter 14

P*resent Day…*

The world came back to her in hazy waves. She could smell coffee and bacon. It was faint, but the scents drifted down to her from the kitchen. She turned her head towards the door and peeled her eyes open. The bedroom door was open, just partially, but it would be enough for the scents to drift down from upstairs.

She let her eyes fall closed again. She didn't know what time it was, but Coop was no longer in bed. She couldn't hear him snoring softly beside her, couldn't feel the heat of his body. She was a little sad about that.

She'd been glad to wake up out of the nightmare with him there. As stubborn as she was, she wasn't above admitting it was nice to have him. She knew she could rely on him. That was the one thing that she'd always been certain about in life. Coop would always be there for her.

She tried to force her eyes open again, fighting against the meds that had made her body numb and her mind foggy. She hated the meds. She hated that she had to fight to get up right now. But there was something to be said about the fact that she felt no pain in her back and shoulders. The fact that she'd actually slept for a few hours.

She got her eyes to open and struggled to sit up. Her limbs felt like they were filled with concrete. She twitched her fingers, reassuring herself that they were still there and still functional as she willed the rest of her body to move.

It felt like it took hours for her to finally sit up in bed, but she was certain it had only been minutes. The fog in her mind was clearing. Her quick glance at the clock told her it was just after seven, which meant she'd actually gotten more hours of sleep than she'd imagined. But three hours was not close to enough. She could feel the tiredness behind her eyes, feel it in how heavy her limbs were. But she wouldn't go back to sleep. Not when she could smell bacon and coffee.

She crawled out of the bed and took a minute to see if her legs would hold her. When she was certain they wouldn't give out, she got to her feet and took a quick assessment of herself in Coop's dresser mirror.

"Well shit," she muttered as she took in the bruising under her bright blue eyes and how pale she was. Her red hair stood up in random spikes that she tried to smooth down, running her fingers through it in frustration.

It took her a moment, but she was eventually satisfied that she didn't look like walking death. "It'll have to do," she mumbled sending her reflection a glare. She cast a glance at the tank top she wore and the track pants she'd stolen from Cooper and gave a shrug that didn't hurt for the first time.

She left the bedroom and followed her nose upstairs to the kitchen. The voices had her hesitating for half a second. Part of her had always felt like she was interrupting when she came upon them like this, like she didn't belong. She pushed that aside and walked into the kitchen with a smile on her face.

"Mum!" She wrapped her arms around the woman seated at the table and pressed a kiss to her cheek. "Well, it's about damn time ya'll showed up."

"Don't sass me, girl." Still, Evie grinned and patted her arm. "Now sit and tell me how you're doin'." She sent a glance at Cooper. "Get the girl a coffee, boyo. Don't just stand there."

Darcy caught his eye roll, but knew that he would do as he was told. There was no arguing with Evelyn McKnight.

Darcy slipped into the chair next to her and gave her a quick scan. She hadn't changed much since Darcy had seen her at the hospital a week ago, but it felt like so much longer now. Her hair had been recently dyed, it looked more vibrant than the last time she'd seen it but the honey blond suited her. It made her cornflower blue eyes stand out, the laugh lines at their corners adding character rather than years to her face.

She was a small woman, always had been, and Darcy had been taller than her before she'd hit high school. But no one was ever really larger than Miss McKnight. She could make you feel like the tiniest ant with just a look, so Darcy had learned early to mind her manners.

She loved Evie like a mother and she'd been Darcy's mother's best friend. But there was always a degree of separation between them. There was always this line they didn't cross. And as she got older she became more and more aware of it.

She smiled at Coop when he set the coffee down in front of her, made just the way she liked it. Then she turned her attention back to Evie. "When did ya'll get in?"

Evie had been doing her own assessment while Coop had been fixing coffee and decided that she looked well enough at the moment. That didn't mean she was well, but it would do for now.

"We got in just after midnight. The house was dead to the world, so figured we'd get up early to start breakfast and see if ya'll would come crawlin' out of the woodwork."

Duncan chuckled from his place at the stove, Coop working beside him. "Who's cookin' breakfast?" he muttered to Coop and got a snicker.

"Don't say that too loud or she'll have both our heads."

"I can hear ya just fine." Evie rolled her eyes. "Now, tell me how you're doin'. Alice won't tell me a damn thing when I call. Somethin' about doctor-patient nonsense."

Darcy smiled. Leave it to Alice to keep things under wraps and then toss her under the bus. "I'm doin' alright. You've seen me worse than this." She waved a hand at her sleep-deprived face. "In theory, it can only get better."

Evie glanced at the burns cascading over her shoulder and down her right arm. They looked better but still she pursed her lips. "You're listenin' to Alice and takin' your meds?"

Darcy nodded knowing if she spoke the lie would be evident in her voice. There was no lying to Miss McKnight.

Evie gave a curt nod. "Good. Well I suppose that covers the awkward part of the morning." She ran a hand over her hair, smiling to herself. "D'ya like the new colour?"

Enjoying the seamless transition, one of Evie's strengths, she smiled. "It's very nice. Did you do it yourself?"

"Of course." She pretended to look offended for half a second. "These old fingers are still capable, as you well know." She reached over and gave Darcy's hair a little tug. "It's not nearly as short as the first time."

Darcy gave a small smile. "I definitely learned that cutting my own hair was not my strength that day."

Among other things, Evie thought, but maintained her smile. "The short hair suits you. It's a shame we had to cut it off again, 'cause the long hair suits you just fine as well. But there was no helpin' it."

"There were rumours my hair smelt pretty terrible." She tried to make light of the fact that she still remembered how it smelt as it burned. "Glad you could fix it for me."

Coop sent her a glance from the stove as he shovelled hashbrowns into a bowl. He caught the tone of her voice even if she was trying to mask it. He saw how her hand shook faintly as she picked up her coffee mug and wanted to curse. He would have if he thought he could get away with it, but his father wasn't above reaming him out for bad language even though he was twenty-two.

"Hey mum, why don't ya see if the girls are alive?" He sent his mother his most winning smile. "Breakfast is almost done and they'll pitch a fit if they miss it."

"Oh don't I know it, boyo." Evie pushed up from the table and headed to the counter to set her cup down. "Be a dear and fix me another tea."

Coop nodded and set the kettle to boil. He also put on a new pot of coffee before he moved over to the table, abandoning his father at the stove. The man could handle it. He took the chair his mother had abandoned and laid his hand overtop Darcy's, which sat on the table, shaking.

"Deep breath in, count to ten, and let it out."

She shot him a glare but she followed his instructions then repeated them for good measure.

"There ya go. That's steadier." He smiled and took a sip of the coffee she'd abandoned. He grimaced at the sugar in it. "I'll never understand how you drink it like that."

"And I'll never understand how you drink it as is." She took her mug back and downed the contents. "Thank you. I thought I was fine, and then I just, I dunno, wasn't."

He shrugged, rocking the chair back on two legs, and knowing his father was pretending to ignore their conversation. "Give it time, Sparky."

"I thought you were callin' me darlin' now." She raised a brow.

"I like to keep ya on your toes."

"You better get four legs on the floor, son, before your mum gets back," Duncan warned as he brought bowls and plates of food to the table.

"Yessir." Coop dropped back down to level, but there was a grin on his face.

Darcy rolled her eyes and glanced at the spread in front of her. She hadn't noticed the extent of what the guys had been working at on the stove. There was bacon, sausages, hashbrowns, scrambled eggs, and even grits. She knew there was yogurt and fresh berries in the fridge, but she doubted anyone other than Beth would be after them. No, the rest of the McKnight clan was not shy away from a good country breakfast.

"Christ, Duncan, are we feeding an army I didn't know ya'll invited?" Darcy reached for a slice of bacon only to have her hand smacked away.

"Now there'll be none of that till everyone else gets down here. And mind your mouth when Evie's around. I may let ya cuss like you're in the garage with Coop, but she'll still tan your hide."

"Don't I know it," Darcy muttered, watching Duncan set the last of the food on the table and go back to the counter to fetch himself a coffee. "How come you're not so much of a hard ass about it?"

He let out a sigh because he knew that she only had so much of a filter, and what she had she reserved for Evie. "I wasn't always a good Catholic boy. Let's just leave it at that."

"What!" Coop looked at his dad then back at Darcy. "What the what?"

Duncan chuckled. "Born and raised Catholic, but let's say I went off the wayward side once I left the nest. Your mother got me back on the straight and narrow, got me goin' to church, but I won't ever buy into it as much as she does."

Coop rested his head on his hands and stared at his father. "My whole life has been a lie."

"Oh, don't be such a drama queen," Duncan scolded, joining them at the table. "And can we move on? Your mother doesn't like me talkin' about this."

"I can't imagine why," Coop muttered but he was grinning. "You rascal you. You owe me a story."

Duncan sighed and looked to Darcy for assistance, but the minute he saw her smile he knew that he'd lost. "Fine, but later."

Coop grabbed Darcy's mug and got up from the table. "I assume you want a refill."

"Please," she chuckled as she heard the footsteps on the stairs.

"She told me there was bacon." Bea wandered into the room, her multicoloured hair a mess atop her head. "If she was lying I'm going back to bed."

And so the chaos began.

Chapter 15

Darcy slipped out of the kitchen while Bea started a rant about the benefits of waking up to breakfast in bed, which had been a perk of her previous relationship at least for a short period of time. The pain was starting to sink back into her shoulders and she wanted to roll them, itch them, and pound against them. But instead she just stepped outside and leaned against the railing.

She knew that putting the cream on after breakfast would help. She'd hit up Alice to do that, leave Coop to socialize some more. She'd kept him away from his family for long enough. She knew that he wouldn't see it like that. But she had always felt bad for the amount of time he'd spent with her over the last few years. If he'd just stayed in Senoia, at the garage, he would be home for dinner every Sunday rather than just visiting on holidays.

She hadn't asked him to come with her. It's true she'd needed a mechanic, one she could trust. But she hadn't asked him to give up his job to follow her on the road. Still, he'd been itching for the road. And as much as working at the shop had been fun for him, it hadn't been enough. She had always known that.

She let the cool breeze from the ocean run over her bare shoulders and enjoyed the sensation. The water was calm in the inlet, but the wind was roughing it up further out. Most of the working boats had already left, but there were a few luxury boats cruising out in the morning light. The inlet held a happy mix.

"Don't let me forget that we have to steal lobster at some point."

Darcy didn't bother glancing back as Coop came up beside her. "Came out for a breather as well?"

"Beth brought up shoes." He visibly shuddered. "I draw the line at shoes."

She laughed. She knew how that conversation could go and couldn't blame him. She liked shoes as much as the next person, but they loved shoes. It was bordering on an addiction.

She glanced over at Coop, leaning against the railing and looking out at the water. "How are we gonna get lobsters back on your bike?"

He glanced over at her, brow furrowed. "I figured we'd take the truck…" He read the fear that lit her eyes the minute he said that and immediately backtracked. "But then I remembered how much Dad likes bartering with Bill so I'll probably send him and mum over to get them anyway."

He watched her relax, could actually see the tension recede, and heard her sigh. "Ya know you'll have to get back in a car eventually," he said softly and caught the sharp look she sent him.

"It's just you and me here, darlin'. I know it's gonna take time, but you'll have to do it eventually."

She relaxed the hands she hadn't realized were gripping onto the railing as though it was her sole lifeline. She drew in a deep breath and let it out, trying to handle the wave of panic that had coursed through her.

"I know," she muttered, not looking at him. Instead, she focused on a small aluminum boat making it's way out of the inlet. It was so peaceful here. That was why she'd wanted to come here after the hospital and not just back to Senoia. Here she felt safe.

"I know," she repeated looking up at him, into those familiar brown eyes. "But for now I figure I'm entitled to a phobia or two." She glanced back towards the house. "Just don't tell them. They're worried enough about me."

"They'll always worry." Coop shrugged running a hand through his shaggy hair. "It's arguably part of their appeal."

Darcy chuckled. "Only you would think so."

* * *

Evie watched them through the open screen door leaning against the railing as if they were completely at ease. Both still sported their sleep clothes and she could see Darcy's burns clearer now from the back.

She pursed her lips as she considered them. Having seen them initially she knew that they had looked worse, but that didn't mean they looked less angry now. She remembered Coop's hands, how red and sore they had been for days. The blisters that had eventually drained and healed. They still sported the red scars, which would fade to white with time. They were still likely stiff and sore, she would imagine. But he wouldn't complain. No, Coop had never been one to complain about much.

She glanced over at Bethany and Beatrice, her twin girls. Her unexpected surprise. They were sitting in the living room now, heads bent together, as different as night and day, deep in conversation. Despite their differences, they had always stuck together. They had always focused on what they shared rather than what made them different.

Across from her Alice chatted with her father, pretending to take interest in his most recent project. She smiled as she tuned into the conversation. Duncan was brilliant, but he'd never been able to tell when his children were indulging him.

"Come now, deary. Let your da finish his breakfast. We'll get started washin' these up."

Alice sent her a grateful glance as she started to gather plates from the table. They worked in silence until they were settled at the sink, the sound of the running water enough to muffle their voices.

"I have no clue what he was talking about," Alice sighed as she took her place drying dishes. It was a familiar set up for them, one they'd had for years.

"None of us do, deary. But it's good of you to listen to him." She smiled as she rinsed off a plate and set it to dry. "He just gets this look about him when he starts talkin' and it seems like a shame to tell him ya don't understand a word."

"He's got to know." Alice shook her head. "I mean they're the most one sided conversations I ever have."

Evie chuckled. "He probably does. But he just gets goin' and then there's no stoppin' him."

"Tell me about it." Alice blew a strand of hair out of her face and once again cursed herself for cutting it. "Now, why did you really drag me over to the sink?"

Evie sent her a sideways glance, keeping her face straight. "I don't know what you're talkin' about."

"Let's skip the dance, mum." She rolled her eyes at the raised brow expression. "You want to know how Darcy's doing." She drew a deep breath in and let it out as a heavy sigh. "I think Mia would have made a better patient."

"If you expected her to be co-operative I question you're judgment." Evie laughed softly. "That lass doesn't have a bone in her body that ain't stubborn as a mule."

"Don't I know it?" Alice placed the plate she was drying on top of the pile. "She doesn't take her meds. She sometimes sleeps, I think. The only thing I know she's doing is applying her cream and doing her range of motion exercises. But she's in pain, physically and mentally. And as far as I can tell, the only one she's letting in is Coop. But that's always been the way with them."

Evie glanced back towards the porch but they were no longer standing there. She could just make out their heads as they crossed the lawn. "They've been attached at the hip since Liv brought her around when they were just wee things."

"And she never really left," Alice mumbled drying another plate.

"Pardon?"

Alice raised her hands in surrender. "I'm not sayin' there's anything wrong with it. Just sayin' she stuck around." She shrugged. "Besides, it was never me who had a problem with her."

Evie went back to washing. "I know Annabelle has never been the fondest of Darcy."

Alice snorted. "That's one way to put it."

"She's got her own family to focus on now. She doesn't need to be botherin' Darcy none."

"Like that'll stop her." Alice sent her mother a sideways glance. "You can pretend we're all little angels but Annie will say what she wants about whatever she's got an opinion on."

"She always had a strong will."

"And a stick up her ass," Alice finished. "And you can scold me for language later, but I'll remind you I'm closer to thirty than twenty now. You'll have to give up eventually."

"You'll never be too old to scold," Evie stated.

Duncan brought his plate over to the counter and offered a small smile. "Are you done with your top secret conversation now?"

Evie raised a brow but smiled. "Not much gets passed you, does it?"

"Not after nearly thirty years of your tricks." He leaned in to press a kiss lightly to her lips and slip his dirty plate into the soapy water. "Thanks for doing the dishes, love."

She glared at him as he walked away to join the twins in the living room. "That man…"

"Still smooth," Alice laughed and gave a nod of approval. Some things never changed, no matter how much time passed.

Chapter 16

Seven Years Ago...

Duncan tapped away at the keyboard trying to control the anger that bubbled just beneath the surface of his resolve. He considered himself to be an even-tempered man, despite his Scottish roots, but there were certain lines that would not be crossed. He drew in a breath and tried to focus on the code in front of him.

He'd heard them when they'd come into the house. It was a big house, but they had to pass the office to get to Coop's room and they'd hardly been quiet. School was out for the summer, and Darcy had convinced her father to let Coop apprentice at the garage. They had been talking excitedly about how great it would be.

Over my dead body, Duncan thought as he hit the keys a little harder than was necessary. He was not going to let his fifteen-year-old son spend his summer at that garage with that man.

He drew in another calming breath and pulled his eyes away from the screen. There was no use to it. He couldn't think straight. Hell, he could barely see straight the way he was feeling right now.

He left his office and went to find the only person who could possible get him out of the mood. The only person who would agree with him.

He found Evie in the kitchen putting a roast pan in the oven. He glanced at the clock and mentally cursed, knowing his wife wouldn't approve of his language. He hadn't realized it was nearly dinnertime already. He hadn't even realized he'd missed lunch.

He closed his eyes and tried to centre himself, tried to calm himself. Before he could get a word out her cornflower blue eyes met his in a stern gaze.

"No." She wagged a finger at him even as the confusion flooded his face. "If you came out 'ere expectin' me to side with you on this, the answer is no."

He just stood there for a moment, mouth slightly open. Finally, he regained his composure. "What?"

"The lad's entitled to a job just as much as anyone else and if he fancies workin' with cars, we have to let him." She held up a hand before he could interrupt. "That's all there is to it."

"I don't get a say in this?" Frustrated that he had once again been out maneuvered by her, he began to pace back an forth.

"You can say whatever ya want. Won't change the way of things." Evie got down a wine glass and poured herself some from the bottle in the fridge. She felt as though the conversation needed it.

"How can you be okay with this?" He threw his hands up in frustration. "You know better than anyone what that man is capable of."

Evie took a sip of her wine, took a moment to respond. "Aye, I do know that. But he's also the best mechanic in the area, has a solid reputation at his job, and has never so much as said a bad word to or about our son. If he wants to 'ave him underfoot for the summer I'm glad to agree."

Duncan opened his mouth and closed it again, gaping like a fish out of water, which is what he felt like at the moment. It was rare that they didn't see eye-to-eye on things, and rarer still that they actually argued. But when it came to the kids that was the only matter that could get their tempers going. And they both had tempers.

"I don't care if he's the best mechanic in the whole Goddamn state of Georgia!" He shouted.

Evie's eyes narrowed. "Don't you dare take the Lord's name in vain. Not in my house."

"Sorry." He knew there was a line there and he had crossed it. He wasn't an overly devout man, but he knew that if he blasphemed another time he'd sleep on the couch.

"But can you understand why I have a problem with this?" He met her gaze, keeping his voice softer now. "I don't want our son having that man as a mentor, as a role model. I barely like the time he spends around him as is."

She nodded. She knew where he was coming from and she had worried about it the entire drive back from town while the kids had chatted excitedly in the backseat. But she knew that if they told him no they would have to justify it, and that was a can of worms she didn't want to open.

"Cooper's a good lad. Strong willed and independent, he is. We've raised him well. You've been a good mentor to him." She smiled, knowing that she was winning him over. "He's got a good head on his shoulders and a good heart."

"But –" He began but she held up her hand again.

"And if you think he doesn't know what kind of man Andy van Dyke is, you're wrong." She glanced towards the ceiling, towards the bedroom where she knew the two of them would be huddled together playing a video game or doing homework. "He's been friends with that girl for almost ten years now. He knows a heck of a lot more than he would ever tell us."

He knew she was right. He knew she was almost always right. But he needed to know that they were on the same page. He needed to know that they were a team. With six kids they needed to be a team. They practically had an army to deal with.

He glanced at her wine and sighed. "I'll take a glass of that, if you don't mind." He took the one she poured for him. "What are you making that smells so delicious?"

She raised a brow. "Are you gonna stay out of your office long enough to eat?"

He grinned taking a sip of the wine. "I think I could be persuaded."

"Pot roast with potatoes and carrots."

He took another sip of the wine. "Yup, that is definitely persuasive."

* * *

Darcy lay on her stomach on Coop's bed her face buried in one of the books she'd been assigned to read over the summer. It was her project to help make up for her poor English grade. The teacher had taken pity on her and given her a summer reading list. It consisted of ten books, all of which she had to write a two page report on.

She turned the page and grumbled. The book was so boring. And there were so many things they could be doing other than this. It was the first day of summer after all.

Coop was stretched out beside her, propped up against his headboard, a book open on his lap. He'd given up reading it several minutes ago. Instead, he was listening. The voices were drifting up faintly through the vents but he could still hear them. His parents didn't realize that he heard almost all of their arguments, and he wasn't about to inform them and ruin his eavesdropping opportunity.

He knew they were arguing about him. He'd known they would the minute Darcy had told him the news, but he didn't really care. Mum had assured him that it was fine to work with Andy for the summer. And mum always got her way. So, he was content to sit and listen while Darcy grumbled over her book.

The shout had them both jolting.

Darcy glanced back at him, their eyes meeting as the shout was met with Evie's firm voice. Darcy bit her bottom lip, closed her book, and crawled up so she was lying beside him on the bed. She snuggled in against his chest and he wrapped an arm around her shoulders. The action and the intimacy of it was so familiar to both of them that they didn't even think about it anymore.

"They're arguing about you, aren't they?" she asked aware that the voices had subsided again. His parents never argued. That was why she liked it so much at the McKnight house; it was the exact opposite of her home in every possible way.

"Nah, they're just hashing some things out." Coop shrugged. "Mum hasn't thrown anything yet so it's not a real argument."

She glanced up at him, and knew that he was making light of it. She clenched her hand into a fist, irritated to find that it was shaking. "Hashing what out?"

"Dad doesn't want me to work for Andy." He sent her a grin. "But mum already agreed so that's that."

"I should have never asked him to take you on for the summer." She shook her head, which basically resulted in her rubbing her face against the soft cotton of his t-shirt. "If I had just left it be then they wouldn't be fighting and it would all be fine."

He heard how her voice shook and tilted her face up to look at him. "This has nothing to do with you, Sparky. And I asked you to get me the damn job, so don't go blaming yourself for anything, ya hear me?"

She blinked those bright blue eyes at him and he could see in them the tears that she wouldn't let fall. "You just wait, at dinner da will be askin' me all about my new job."

"How do you know?"

He smiled at her. "It's just their way." He gave her hair a tussle before she could squirm away. "Now, how about I kick your ass at Donkey Kong before we get recruited to set the table."

She sent him a glare as she tried to straighten her hair. "You're on."

Chapter 17

Present Day...

Coop looked under the hood of Dr. Dillon's pickup truck and heaved a sigh. Every inch of the engine was covered in grime and there had been an ominous clunking sound coming from underneath it when he'd taken it for a drive. He would have thought that someone as meticulous as Dr. Dillon, family physician, would be more careful about his vehicle. But apparently it sat low on his priority list.

He cursed softly as he wiped away some of the grime to get a better look at what was going on in the engine. He was pretty sure he knew the cause of the clunking. But before he could even bother with that he had to get the grime off, check the fluids, and make sure all the lines were fine. He had zero confidence that this vehicle had been checked in the last five years.

"Screw family discount," he muttered trying to unscrew the oil cap. "I'm gonna bill you out the ass for this, Dillon."

"Be sure you give him the bill after your next appointment." Duncan stepped into the garage a smile lighting his hazel eyes bringing out the creases at the corners. "He may not be so gentle after he sees all those zeros."

Coop chuckled even though he hadn't seen Dr. Dillon since he was a kid. He gave a hoot as he finally got the oil cap off. "Stubborn SOB."

Duncan peered into the engine with interest. "You would think a guy who could write code for NASA could figure out what you're holding in your hand."

"A guy who can do that doesn't need to know that this is an oil cap." Coop paused then glanced over at his father. "Wait, you coded for NASA."

Duncan shrugged and waved a hand dismissively. "A few years ago they called me up." He grinned. "That's how I got the hat."

"I figured you just picked that up at the store or something."

"Nah, that's an official NASA hat," he chuckled. "Now, why exactly are you charging Dr. Dillon out the ass?"

"Because…" Coop pulled out the dipstick and wasn't remotely surprised that it came out almost dry. "Dr. Dillon is probably the worst truck owner in the Basin."

"You know he doesn't actually live in the Basin," Duncan corrected and received a glare for his effort. "Just saying."

"Regardless, this truck is a disgrace." Coop struggled to get another cap off. "I'm surprised it hasn't died on him or exploded." He grunted with the effort but finally got it off. "Yup, it probably should have exploded."

Duncan watched his son work with the curiosity of a man who understood numbers more than physical objects. He could appreciate the competent movements, the methodology of them, even if he didn't fully understand their purpose. And every now and then it bothered him that another man had taught his son all of this, but he tried not to linger on those thoughts. He tried to focus on the fact that his son was growing into a man that he was proud of.

"How many jobs have you lined up since you got here?"

Coop glanced over at his dad and sighed. "Under ten so far. So, that's better than the last time I came home."

"This always has been home to you, hasn't it?" Duncan glanced around, contemplatively.

"Senoia has my heart, but my soul is here in the Basin," he replied as he took another part from under the hood.

Duncan chuckled at the familiar line. "Well, you should know better than to wander into town if you want any peace and quiet. The minute they know you're here there is no escape."

"Spoken like a true hermit." Coop knew he got a glare for that one, but he was wrist deep in grime and didn't care. "Speaking of town, Bill O'Hare has some lobsters for you as long as mum brought her jarred peaches."

"Is that so?" Duncan rocked back on his heels, hands in his pockets so he wouldn't touch anything. "When'd you see him?"

"Same day I picked up this job." He emerged from under the hood and wiped his hands on the rag he'd tucked in his back pocket. "Another hazard of going into town is you see people as well as get jobs."

"I thought you were gonna take it easy for a bit once you got up here. I thought that was the whole point."

Coop shrugged. "Darcy was gettin' cabin fever so we went over to Dave's Place for lunch. I forgot how dangerous that place was."

"And how are you doing?" Duncan picked a wrench up off the workbench, tested its weight and set it back down. That was the real reason he'd wandered out to the garage. He wanted to get a read on how his son was handling all of this. After all, Darcy hadn't been the only one injured two months ago.

"I'm fine." Coop went back under the hood and rummaged around for a few minutes. When he reemerged his father was still looking at him intently. "Honestly, Da, I'm fine.

All healed up." He waved his grime covered hands, dirt and grease covering any trace of the fire that had marked his flesh.

"Don't pull that crap with me," he warned, his voice steady.

Coop knew the tone and sighed. "Alright, maybe fine isn't the best word to use. But I'm doin' a hell of a lot better than Darcy. So, don't worry about me. I can handle my own shit."

"It's my job to worry about you."

"And you do a fine job of it. But I'm tellin' you not to bother." He ran a hand through his hair, effectively spreading the grime through it as well.

Duncan knew that look well. The frustration and exhaustion warred on his son's face, coupled with a need to say something but an uncertainty of what. He felt like he had lived with that expression on his face for most of his younger years. He closed the distance between them and laid a hand on Cooper's shoulder.

"Why don't you tell me what's on your mind, son?"

Coop met his gaze for a moment and wondered if he could. He'd never had a problem talking to his father. His mum pushed and questioned, but with his father it had always been easy conversation, it had always been simple. He looked into that familiar face, barely touched by age though he would be fifty this year.

He considered it for half a second but merely shook his head. "There's too much for a simple conversation, Da." When he watched those hazel eyes flood with worry he sighed. "I just have to figure a few things out on my own. I'll let you in on it when I get it all sorted."

Duncan wondered how much of his clouded mind had to do with the red head asleep on the couch right now. He gave his son's shoulder another pat and then leaned over to glance under the hood of the truck. "So, how about you tell me what exactly you're doing here."

Cause that went so well last time, Coop thought but he was glad for the distraction and the change of topic. So, adopting the role of instructor, a rare occurrence when his father was around, Coop began shop class 101.

* * *

She felt the wool blanket scratch against her burnt shoulder as she rolled over and ground her teeth together. It didn't hurt so much as it felt like someone scrapping nails across her skin. She opened her eyes and glanced at the Afghan someone had placed over her and that she, no doubt in her drug induced state, had cocooned herself in.

The familiar sounds of *Jeopardy!* filled the room. Darcy glanced over at Beth who was curled up in the overstuffed armchair next to the window overlooking the bay. The woodstove in the corner was unlit, but it made the room toasty on a cold winter day. And the rocking chair next to it was where Evie often sat while she worked on her knitting. It, like every other room in the house, always felt welcoming.

Beth was watching the screen across from her intently, a cup of steaming tea in her hands, and her legs tucked beneath her.

"What is the duodecimal system?" she stated right before the contestant on the TV replied the same thing. She made a notation on the notepad beside her and went back to watching the TV.

"Are you winning?" Darcy pushed herself up slowly, well aware that her limbs didn't want to cooperate.

Beth glanced over and grinned. "Doing better than these shmucks." She rolled her eyes. "Who is Donald Trump?" she answered the next question seamlessly before the contestant could and made another notation. "They really need to make this stuff harder."

"Or you need to stop reading encyclopedias in your spare time," Darcy laughed as she stood to fold the blanket. "Why do they call this an Afghan?"

Beth didn't even glance over at her. "Because Europeans adopted the weaving technique from the people of Afghanistan."

"Huh," Darcy set the blanket aside and moved closer to the TV, sitting on the arm of Beth's chair. "How long was I out for?"

Beth glanced up at her, took in the shadows under her bright eyes. "Not nearly long enough."

The intro song cued them back in after the commercial break and they waited for the next series of questions. Darcy forgot how much she had enjoyed this. She was not a trivia buff like Beth, but she held her own in a round of *Jeopardy!* And she was doing pretty well at the moment. It helped a little that this round had a whole section on NASCAR.

"Who is Tony Stewart?" she stated before Beth even had a chance to guess. Darcy glanced at her triumphantly. "You might at well write off this column, Beth. I'm gonna beat you to the punch on every one."

"We'll see about that." Beth leaned forward and tried to read off the next question before they finished reading it out loud.

"Who is Jeff Gordon?" Darcy grinned as the contestant also answered correctly. She caught Beth's glare and gave a small shrug. "You know everything, can't you just give me this one thing?"

"No," Beth grumbled but it was nice to have company. She was used to watching *Jeopardy!* reruns by herself in the early hours of the morning. Her studying habits from school hadn't quite disappeared even though she was now into an internship. She rarely slept, she worked too much, and she consumed as much knowledge as she could. *Jeopardy!* was just one way to expedite the process.

Darcy laughed, content with her place on the arm of the chair and with Beth's companionship. Beth was the quiet one, the one that no one ever really noticed, at least when Bea was around. But Darcy had always liked her. She'd never fostered the same friendship that she had with Bea, with her twin, but they were amicable. Beth had always been too focused for their shenanigans. In many ways, she still was.

"Who is Miss Universe?"

They both glanced over as Bea came into the room, a loaded tray in hand. "What?" She raised a brow. "I know things too. Well, things about fashion and art and music. Not really useful things."

She set the tray down and passed a mug of coffee to Darcy. "Mum figured you were awake from the way you both were yellin' at the TV."

"We weren't yelling." Beth rolled her eyes.

"Whatever. It's a weird hobby, if you ask me."

"Nobody did."

Bea ignored that. "Anyhow, she made up some sandwiches. Alice said the meds make you feel like crap, but said I was to make sure you eat."

"Did they go somewhere?" Darcy picked up a sandwich and took a bite. She hadn't realized how hungry she was. Hell, she didn't even know what time it was.

Bea shrugged and dropped down on the coffee table next to the tray. She picked up a sandwich and studied it before taking a bit. "They said something about peaches and lobsters then went out the door. So, to hell if I know."

"Bill O'Hare is trading your mum lobsters for peaches," Darcy muttered absently as she ate her sandwich. She paused when she felt both sets of eyes on her. "What?"

"How do you know this?" They asked in unison. Darcy had always found it eerie when they did that.

"Bill stopped Coop and I at Dave's Place and said he would trade lobsters for peaches. I assume Coop told your mum, which is why they're out now." She shrugged and tried to hide the grimace. The drug-numbed pain was returning. "Which means we're having lobster for dinner tomorrow."

"Fuck yeah!" Bea did a happy dance from her seat on the table.

"You're lucky mum isn't around or you'd get a smack." Beth had almost given up on *Jeopardy!* but she still had half an eye on the TV and was mentally answering the questions.

"I know when to hold my tongue and watch my language. It's this one who has to worry."

"Hey!" Darcy gave her a narrowed eye look. "I behave."

"Uh huh, and I'm a saint." Bea giggled. "Just keep your head down once Annie shows up and your temper under control and we'll all be good."

Darcy sighed. "She still doesn't like me?"

Bea gave her a sympathetic smile and patted her knee. "She doesn't like anyone. It's part of her charm." She stood up and stretched her arms above her head. "Now, how about we ditch this trivia nonsense and watch one of the many semi-legally obtained films I brought back with me."

"Any of them have half naked men in them?" Beth glanced at her sister.

"Some of them have full naked men in them."

"Well then, count me in." Beth switched off the TV and swung out of the chair. "But I vote we watch in our bedroom.

Da has a habit of walking in exactly when the good scenes happen."

Bea laughed, remembering the many times it had happened in the past. "Good call."

"Popcorn?" Darcy raised a brow

"Nah, I've got chocolate upstairs. C'mon before the guys get back and try to distract us."

"You don't have to tell me twice."

Chapter 18

The house was fully lit up when they pulled into the driveway. Annabelle McKnight was glad to see that they hadn't gone to sleep even thought it was well after ten in the evening. She had been fairly certain that they would wait up for her, but there was still a sense of relief that washed over her at seeing the lights. She was home.

It didn't matter that she lived in Atlanta now or that she'd spent half her life in Georgia. This house would always be home to her. The Basin would always be home. And she was glad that she could bring her family here even if it meant having to deal with the rest of her crazy family.

She glanced back at her daughter, asleep in her car seat. Caught in between two and three, Mia was her own little person now. She was feisty. She knew some words and she wasn't afraid to use them. And she made her mother proud every day.

Drew Coleman, her husband of three years now, laid a hand on her arm. "Are we just gonna sit here all night or we gonna go inside and say hello?"

She glanced over at him and caught his smile. A quick flash of white teeth against dark flesh. She resisted the urge to sigh and instead nodded before getting out of the car.

It took them several minutes to coordinate things, never in her life would she have thought a child needed so much luggage until she'd had one. Finally, they were mounting the steps to the front door and heading into the house.

"Ya'll have five minutes to say hello to Mia before I put her straight to bed." Anna offered as means of a greeting as she strolled into the crowded kitchen, toddler on her hip. All eyes swung to her and smiles broke out across the room.

"We didn't expect you till morning," Duncan said from behind his laptop but his voice was happy.

"Ya'll can see her tomorrow," Evie announced getting up from her chair and giving her second oldest a kiss on the cheek. "Come here to nana." She took Mia from Anna's hip and rested her on her own. "I'll see she gets put down for the night. You settle in." Evie took the diaper bag and headed towards the stairs before anyone could protest.

Anna didn't think she had the energy too. She set her bag by the stairs and accepted the cup of tea from her father. She knew it was too late to drink coffee but she really wanted one.

She leaned back against the counter because she couldn't possibly sit any longer and scanned the faces gathered in the kitchen. "Charlie not here yet?"

"Far as we know she should show up in the morning," Alice shrugged. "Something about a last minute practice."

"Sounds about right." Anna took a sip of the tea and burnt her tongue. "I'm here for 36 hours. No more no less, so don't try to talk me into staying beyond that. It was hard enough getting off the time I did."

"Wouldn't dream of asking you to stay longer," Bea muttered and accepted the glare sent at her.

"Now, I'd love to catch up, but we've both put in full work days, wrestled a toddler onto a plane and into a rental, and then drove here. So, it'll all have to wait till morning." She glanced over at her husband, daring him to argue.

Drew gave an easy smile, his brown eyes laughing. "Yes, it's been a long day. It's lovely to see you all again, but goodnight."

"Yes, goodnight." Anna nodded, scanning the faces once more before landing on Darcy's. "Oh, and Darcy?" She waited for those bright blue eyes to meet hers. "I'm glad you're okay."

With that she left the room, hoping that she could sleep until dawn. Praying that her daughter would let her.

Darcy watched her leave with a mixture of relief and sadness. She'd never been on the best of terms with Annie. She never fully understood why. There was seven years between them so they'd never been in school together. The most time they'd spent together had been at the McKnight house. And other than the odd time she'd had to babysit Darcy and Coop when Alice had been busy, Annie had stayed away from her.

She wondered if Annie really didn't like anyone much, like Bea said. But Darcy had seen her interact with her husband, who was probably the kindest man alive. And she'd seen her interact with her daughter. The woman was capable of being nice, she was just picky.

Darcy had no clue what she'd done to offend Coop's older sister and she figured she'd probably never know, not unless she asked directly. And she was much too stubborn to do that. She'd rather deal with the dark looks than directly confront the problems. It wasn't that she didn't like confrontation, given the right situation. She just didn't want to disrupt the one peaceful place she had in her life.

"Well, she always did know how to make an entrance." Bea took a sip of the beer she had in front of her. "At least Drew was smiling. Though that hunk of burnin' love is always smiling."

"Beatrice!" This came from Duncan who was behind his laptop at the head of the table.

"What?" She rolled her eyes. She had long ago given up on being subtle around her father. "I'm just saying, Annie landed herself one heck of an attractive man. Though how she did it I will never know."

"She is a bit of an ice queen," Beth said contemplating a piece of broccoli she'd just picked up. "Maybe she's great in bed."

"Bethany!" Duncan's face had changed to a nice shade of red.

"What?" She shrugged, sounding just like her twin. "It's not like you don't know they have sex. They have a kid."

"That doesn't mean any of us want to think about their sex lives, or any of yours for that matter," Coop countered and watched his father's face deepen another shade. "Sorry."

"I knew I should have put in headphones," he muttered staring intently at his screen.

Darcy chuckled. This was the part of the family she loved. Everyone at the table understood her. And they never pushed her. This was the light and playful aspect that she sought out when she visited the McKnight house. This was the peace she only found here.

"Oh, don't pretend you're a prude, da." Bea grinned as he continued to blush. "You had six kids, after all."

This had everyone laughing and Duncan grabbing his computer and getting up from the table. "I surrender. Tell your mum I'll be on the porch licking my wounds."

Darcy watched him wander out with a smile on her face. "It's too easy to get him riled up."

Coop, who was still a few shades of red, shrugged. "Some things shouldn't be talked about at the dinner table."

Bea rolled her eyes again. "You're as bad as him. Like you're so innocent. Or should I start namin' names?" She enjoyed that he blushed a bit more at that. "Anyway, we were talking about the ice queen before we got sidetracked and her uber attractive king."

"Where did she even find him?" Darcy asked. She'd been out of the loop of family politics for the last few years, except for the basics.

"He's a kindergarten teacher in Atlanta, of all things. She met up with him on a case she was working." Bea grinned. "From the way he tells it, and oh you should hear him tell it."

"Focus Beatrice," Beth sighed.

"Anyhow, he says he was smitten from the get go and, of course, Annie wouldn't give him the time of day. But he's a patient and persistent fella."

"Looks the type," Darcy said, considering her impressions of Drew the past few times she'd met him.

"Worked out for him in the end." Bea shrugged a dreamy expression on her face. "And to hell if Mia isn't the cutest thing."

"She is indeed." Darcy thought of the mocha-skinned toddler with her dark hair a curly mess that Evie had carted up to bed. "I was sad that I missed the wedding and the christening."

The faces around the table softened and Bea laid a hand over hers. "You had things to attend to. None of us blame you for not being there."

Annie might, Darcy thought but she didn't bother saying it. Even she didn't think Annie was that petty. Given the choice, she would have picked a wedding over a funeral, but there had been no avoiding it or the funeral the following year that had coincided with Mia's christening. Bad timing. Her life was full of it.

"Well, I think that's my cue to go to sleep." Darcy gave a small smile, feeling the little bit of peace she'd gained from the earlier conversation slip away from her. She knew that she wouldn't sleep tonight. She wouldn't let herself wake up screaming. She wouldn't risk the rest of the house hearing that.

But right now she needed to be alone, with her thoughts, with her memories.

Chapter 19

Darcy didn't sleep. It took a great deal of effort and even more caffeine, but when she saw the sun creep up over the inlet she was relieved. She had sent Coop to bed hours ago. He had tried to stay awake with her to keep her company, but she knew that he'd barely slept the night before. He was dead on his feet and today was going to be chaos. It was best that he get some sleep.

She leaned against the railing of the porch and watched the sunrise. The coffee at her elbow was steaming hot against the chill of the morning but she loved it. In comparison to Georgian summers, the weather here was beautiful. She rarely broke a sweat and the ocean breeze was always refreshing.

Her light tank top kept most of the weight off her burns and the loose cotton pants she wore barely rubbed against the graft site on her thigh. It was the best she could ask for. She'd put cream on as best she could a few hours ago and done her range of motion exercises, but she would need Alice to get the spots she'd missed.

She looked forward to the day that they didn't hurt when touched. The day that she could wear normal clothes again. The day she could wear a bra. She was really looking forward to that day. She felt uncomfortable walking around the house with everyone in her baggy shirt and no bra. Not that she had the biggest chest in the world, but still.

She rolled her shoulders and picked up the coffee mug. The Tylenol she'd taken earlier was taking the edge off but everything still had a dull throb to it. She thought about taking one of her prescription meds. She knew that she could probably get in a few hours of sleep before things started to get hectic, but she didn't want to miss it. And she definitely didn't want to wake up screaming in a house full of people.

No, it would be Tylenol all day, despite her promise to Bea. She couldn't afford to sleep through the day. And she definitely couldn't afford the nightmares. She would just have to make due with the caffeine she had. She didn't think she could have slept anyhow with the weight of the pain on her system right now. Every breath hurt, but it was nothing she was not becoming accustomed to.

She heard the front door open and glanced back through the house. She hadn't heard the car pull up but, then again, she hadn't been listening for one. She'd been lost in her own thoughts. It took a few moments but she saw the familiar figure of Charlotte McKnight wander out towards the porch.

"I wondered if anyone would be awake." Charlie took the coffee from Darcy's hands and gulped half of it. "Bleh, how do you drink it like that?"

"Well, usually I actually drink it," Darcy chuckled taking the mug back. "It's good to see you, Charlie."

She grinned, a winning smile that would have even the most reserved guy weak in the knees. "Glad to see you're still in one piece. I would have come out to see you but I had games on the other side of the country for the last four months."

"It's no matter. I was hardly in a state for visitors."

"That's fair. You're entitled to your privacy at a time like that."

Darcy watched her lean against the railing, facing the house instead of the inlet. She was a ball of energy. She always had been. Her brown hair was pulled back into a long French braid that swung passed her shoulder blades and her brown eyes were the same as Cooper's. She was the only one to share his eyes. Her 5'10 frame was athletic, kept in shape by a rigorous routine and constant practice. But she was one of the friendliest people Darcy had ever met.

"Did you just fly in?"

"Yeah," Charlie replied still examining the house, her mind wandering. "I caught an afternoon flight out of San Fran with a layover in Toronto. It was the only way I could get here for the morning."

"So, you haven't slept and you've had about twelve million coffees?"

Charlie shot her that winning smile again. "Something like that."

"Well, join the club on that one."

Charlie glanced over at her as she sipped coffee. She almost asked why Darcy hadn't slept, but her training had taught her not to interfere. Darcy wasn't her patient. She wasn't responsible for her rehabilitation. And if Darcy didn't want to sleep, that was her business. She'd learned a great deal about the benefits of privacy in the last few years.

"How about we head in and put on a fresh pot of coffee?" Darcy suggested taking Charlie's silence as a sign that her mind had begun to wander again. She was always off thinking about something or other. Very rarely did she stay fixated on the conversation at hand.

"Sure." Charlie gave her an assessing look. She was in pain. That much was clear on her face and her grip on the coffee mug, but her voice was steady. Charlie had seen many levels of pain in her kinesiology/rehabilitative therapy training. She knew the signs. And Darcy was definitely in pain.

Charlie followed her into the house, watching the stiffness in her walk. She favoured her right leg when she walked. Her shoulder and neck were exceptionally tense and her teeth were clenched. Charlie filed that away but didn't comment. She would talk to Alice about it.

"You're the last one to arrive." Darcy glanced back at her as she set about making a fresh pot of coffee. "Well, other than the mob of people who will show up today. But they don't really count."

"It'll be nice to see the whole family." Charlie watched her reach for the coffee and suck in a breath at the way her shirt rubbed against her burns. Yet she continued making the coffee as if nothing had happened.

"Your family is more like an army when it comes to size." Darcy sent her a smile trying to swallow the wave of nausea that had just washed over her. "Not to mention the fact that everyone from the Basin will wander over eventually."

"At least they all bring food." Charlie hopped up on the counter. "I can't wait to get my hands on all of the food."

"Speaking of which, we should probably start breakfast if we're awake. I give it another half hour before everyone starts moving."

Charlie jumped down and rubbed her hands together. "It's been too long since I've got to cook any real food. I call frying the bacon."

Darcy held her hands up in surrender, a grin on her face. "It's all yours."

* * *

Cooper rolled over and caught himself before he fell out of bed. He laid there for a moment, his heart racing, and his eyes searching for something to ground him to reality. He'd been buried in the nightmare and unable to find an escape. The fear still felt like a family of snakes wrestling in his stomach.

He drew in a steadying breath and let it out slowly. He knew he was in his bedroom. He hadn't been sure of that a minute ago, but he was grounded again. A minute ago he'd been in the pits watching it all happen. A minute ago he'd felt his heart drop even as his feet carried him towards the crash. A minute ago he'd been at the worst day of his life again.

He glanced over at the empty bed beside him. He knew that Darcy hadn't gone to bed. Despite his protests, she would have stayed up to avoid the very thing that had jolted him awake. He tried not to acknowledge the small part of him that was sad she hadn't been there to wake up to. Instead, he focused on the fact that she hadn't slept since her afternoon nap and today was going to be chaos.

With a sigh, he got out of bed and opted for a shower before wandering upstairs. The house was still fairly silent, so he figured his chances of getting hot water were still fairly good. A hot shower and then coffee. That was his plan. Then he would worry about how he was going to get through Canada Day without injury.

He indulged in the hot water while he had it. The one sign that the rest of the house was still asleep, but when he reached to turn the knobs off his hands still shook a little. He closed them into fists and drew in a deep breath. He needed to get himself together before he faced off with everyone today.

He dressed quickly, ignoring the fact that his heart was racing and that his mind wanted to go back to the dream he'd been woken from. He didn't want to think about that day. He didn't want to think about the accident or what had nearly happened.

He headed out the sliding doors before he even registered he was going outside. In jeans and plain t-shirt he wandered onto the lawn, enjoying the feeling of the cool grass on his bare feet and the ocean breeze. He drew in a deep breath and ran his hands through his hair.

"Ahhhhh!" He squeezed his eyes shut and tried to ride out the panic as it coursed through him. It was one thing to coach

Darcy through it. To tell her it was going to be alright. It was another thing entirely to be drowning in it himself.

He dropped down to his knees, hands buried in his hair, and fell forward until his face rested firmly in the grass. He was glad that everyone else was asleep, because he knew he was making a scene in the backyard at the moment.

He just needed a moment. He needed to collect himself. He couldn't be the one falling apart right now. Darcy needed him to be the stable one. The one she could lean on when her reality was crumbling. He needed to get his feet under him before he could go inside.

He drew in another deep breath, smelling the grass and dirt with it, before he slowly made his way back to an upright position. The wet ground was soaking through the knees of his jeans but he didn't care. They would dry out and they would likely get dirtier before the end of the day.

"Well fuck," he muttered, pushing himself to his feet and brushing the worst of the debris from his knees. His hands were barely shaking now, but he didn't quite believe he could go back inside. So, he wandered towards the garage instead. He'd work until he couldn't think anymore, until he didn't remember the nightmare. Then he would let his day start.

Chapter 20

Seven Years Ago...

Darcy sat on top of the tool chest, her foot tapping absently to the rock music that was blasting from the garage speakers. Usually it was country but her father had made an exception for Coop. He was the only person her father would ever make an exception for.

She took a sip of the beer that she was still six years too young to drink. But her father didn't care. She had learned early on that if he handed her a beer she should accept it without question. She wasn't about to piss him off and she wasn't about to make him regret having a daughter.

So, she would sip her beer but she would only have the one. And she would never tell mama about it. That was the other rule. What happened at the garage stayed there.

She watched Coop and her dad fiddle away at the bike he'd bought just last week. He'd been so excited about the Honda Rebel. It was his project. Any logical teenager wanted a car, but Coop wanted a motorcycle. And he wanted to make it run with his own hands.

Darcy had her own project car, a little Honda Civic that her father had picked up cheap and was helping her fix up. It wasn't pretty, but it was a start. And she was putting in her time on it when she wasn't at the diner or at school. There was a satisfaction in fixing something yourself. She could understand why Coop wanted to do it. But she still didn't understand the motorcycle.

"Cocksucker!"

She watched her father throw the wrench across the floor and bring his grease-covered thumb to his mouth.

"Did it bite you?" She asked, hopping off of the tool chest and wandering over to them. She tried to stay out of their way when they were working, not because she was useless around the shop, but because Coop was there to learn.

"Took a good chunk out." Andy held up his thumb so Darcy could see the chunk missing before the blood started pooling again and he quickly returned it to his mouth.

"Well give me a sec and I'll grab the first aid kit." She sent Coop a grin before running off to the office to retrieve it.

"You couldn't pick a cooperative machine, eh?" Andy mumbled around his thumb.

"No, sir," Coop replied examining his bike lovingly. He could see it done in his mind. It had been a steal for a hundred bucks. His mum was still angry with him for it, but he knew she would come around. He didn't want the nice hybrid they offered to buy him. He wanted this bike, and he wanted to build it with his own two hands.

"Reminds me of the car I had when I was your age." Andy sat back on his heels, his thumb still in his mouth. "That old Ford tried to kill me at least a dozen times before I got it on the road. And even then it tried a few more times."

"How long did ya have it for?"

"Still have it." He nodded his head towards the Ford F-100 parked out behind the garage. "If you build it right it will last forever."

"Sorry it took so long." Darcy opened the first aid kit as she crouched down next to her father. "Took me forever to find the damn thing."

She glanced up from her process of taking gauze from the kit and looked from one man to the other. "I've missed something, haven't I?"

"Just sharing some wisdom," Andy stated, a small smile on his face. He looked over at his daughter and the smile only faltered slightly. "Now, why don't you be a doll and wrap this up so I can get back to it."

"Sure thing." Darcy set to work and pretended that she didn't notice the way his smile dropped away when he looked at her. She would put that image away with all the other negative ones she had of him. Right now he was her father, and right now she loved spending time with him.

* * *

Present Day...

The rock music blasted from the speakers of the small stereo and Coop tapped his foot along to it. He sung the words under his breath while he tinkered with the engine above him. Dr. Dillon's truck was coming along. The clunking noise had been some worn ball joints, which he would have to order in after the holiday. But he'd managed to change the fluids and the lines looked fine.

He was doing a good job at distracting himself from his morning breakdown. He'd known that burying himself in an engine would do it. It always seemed to.

He had a ratchet in one hand and was about to check something when he felt a shoe hook under his heel. He had enough time to curse before he was jerked out from underneath the car.

"Goddamnit!" He sat up when he was clear of the bumper and looked at the individual responsible. The smile spread across his face immediately. "Well, I should have known."

Charlie grinned and handed over the mug of coffee. "Peace offering?" She watched him down half of it in one shot. "Darcy said I'd find you in here."

Coop raised a brow but merely continued drinking the coffee as Charlie wandered around the space. She never could sit still, he thought watching her. She was a ball of energy all the time.

"She's inside making breakfast," Charlie continued as she picked up a screwdriver and spun it idly. "I was helping her," she shot him a look, "until she sent me out here with coffee."

"Hey, I didn't say anything. And I'm grateful for the coffee." He hadn't realized how much he needed it until it was in his hands and now the mug was nearly empty. "Anyone else awake?"

"Not when I left, but it sounded like people were stirring upstairs." She shrugged. "I suppose Mia will be waking up soon. And mum and da always get up early. Bea will be the last one up."

"She always is." Coop downed the rest of his coffee and looked longingly into the cup. "I suppose I have to go inside to get more of this."

"One time delivery."

"Damn." He got up from his crawler board and stretched. "Is there bacon inside?"

Charlie gave him a bland look as she exchanged the screwdriver for an adjustable wrench. "Is there ever not bacon?"

He merely shrugged and started putting away his tools. If there was one thing Andy had drilled home with him it was that everything had to be put away before you could leave the garage. It was a habit he strived to maintain.

"So, what's new with you, sis? Still soaking up that Cali sun?"

"Every chance I get." She hopped up onto the workbench and watched him work. She had always enjoyed watching him in the garage. It was the only place he seemed completely comfortable. "Clearly you're still up to your elbows in grease."

"It's good for the skin." He smiled when she laughed. Out of all of his sisters, Charlie had always been the easiest to be around. Perhaps it was because they were only two years apart or perhaps it was her quiet, assessing nature. She was never quick to judge but she was always quick to laugh.

"I'll keep that in mind next time I pay for a spa day."

He curled his lip in disgust. "You mean those places where they put mud on your face and wrap you in seaweed and crap? You go to that?"

She rolled her eyes. "I've been known to attend. Sometimes it's nice to pamper yourself." She chuckled as he shuddered. "I'd never been before Nate got me a day pass for my birthday, but it's actually really fun."

Coop glanced over at her, a sly expression on his face. "And who exactly is Nate?"

She realized her mistake the moment she looked at his face. She'd been busy thinking of hot stone massages and not paying attention to what came out of her mouth. "Damnit."

"Uh huh." He stopped putting away his tools and leaned against the workbench next to her. "So, who's Nate?"

"You can't tell mum."

He gave her his best attempt at an offended expression. "Like I would ever."

"Cooper Joseph Douglas McKnight, you swear to me that you will not tell mum or I'm not saying a thing." She crossed her arms, reminding him of a much younger version of her.

He grinned and held out his pinky. "Pinky swear, Charlie." They shook on it. "Now, tell me who the hell Nate is."

She bit her lower lip and let out a sigh. "He's my boyfriend and has been for about a year now."

"A year!" He threw his arms up for emphasis.

"Calm down, Coop."

"I talked to you at Christmas and you said nothing. And nothing at Thanksgiving." He gave her a narrow-eyed look. "I feel so lied too."

"Oh, fuck off." She rolled her eyes and he laughed. "Like you ever told us about your girlfriends. Darcy's the only one you've ever brought home and its not like there's anything going on there."

He wasn't about to touch that statement with a ten-foot pole. "Well, it's not like they were serious relationships." He gave a half shrug and went back to putting away tools. "You know how mum is with relationships."

"Exactly!" Charlie hopped off the bench and began to pace. She needed to move. "Mum has this crazy notion that we're set on marrying any lad or lass we bring home. I mean, how am I supposed to know if I want to marry him or not."

She ran her hands over her face then threw her arms up in frustration. "I mean, I've only known him for a year. And I'm away a lot and so is he, with work. How am I supposed to know if it's serious? I definitely wasn't bringing him home for this." She waved her arms to indicate the space around her.

"No, definitely don't do that."

"Fuck, Coop." Charlie sat down on the floor halfway through pacing and brought her hands to her mouth. "I'm in love with Nate."

Coop looked over at his sister and sighed. He walked over to her, took her hands, and pulled her to her feet. Then wrapped her in a hug.

"What the hell am I supposed to do, Coop?" she mumbled against his shoulder.

"Well, I would suggest telling him what you just told me for starters." He pulled her back and held her by the shoulders so he could meet her gaze, so he could look into the same eyes he saw in the mirror. "Then I suggest you bring him to meet the family."

"I don't know about that..."

"Nope, he has to come now." He slung a companionable arm around her shoulder and headed out of the garage. He would worry about the rest of his mess later. "Now, you have until we get back to the house to tell me some more about him."

"Coop..."

"Don't test me, Charlie." He sent her a sideways glance. "I've barely had any coffee."

She laughed, as he knew she would, and began her story.

Chapter 21

Darcy slipped out of the kitchen. It wasn't hard to do. People were busy passing Mia around the table, commenting on how much she'd grown since they'd seen her at Easter. When she'd left Cooper had been bouncing her on his knee and telling his sister that her daughter was a great deal nicer than she was.

Darcy smiled at the statement. She hadn't thought that Anna was in a bad mood that morning. But every time she would settle on that thought she'd receive an unprovoked glare from the older woman. And every comment she'd made had been ignored or talked over. She'd slipped out before Mia could be passed to her. She didn't want to see Anna's expression if Darcy got a chance to hold her child.

That hadn't been her only reason for exiting the room. She'd spent the fifteen minutes that everyone had been awake making sure the table was full and everyone had what they needed. Charlie had been right there with her playing hostess. They'd taken on the job since they were the first ones awake knowing full well someone else would have to do the dishes.

She hadn't said a word to Coop yet. She'd caught his concerned glances as he downed two more cups of coffee after the one she'd sent out for him. She didn't need his worry right now. She just needed to get through the morning. Luckily Bea had been there to distract him until everyone else had made their way downstairs.

She left the kitchen now and headed upstairs as fast as her legs would take her. She could feel the little bit that she had eaten for breakfast rolling in her stomach. She had been fighting the nausea for the last ten minutes, but she knew that if she didn't make it to the bathroom soon she was done for.

There was a bathroom on the main floor, but there was no way she was going there. No way she was letting everyone in the kitchen hear her throw up her breakfast. There was no way she was letting them know that she was in so much pain it was making her sick.

She closed the upstairs bathroom door and turned the lock. She hated locking doors, shutting them out. It reminded her too much of her locked bedroom door as a child. It made her think that there was something terrible on the other side of the door that she had to keep out. But no, she was the something terrible this time. She needed to keep herself away from the rest of them, from the happiness that was downstairs.

She barely made it to the toilet before the toast and bacon she'd eaten while cooking came back on her. Her back muscles spasmed as she dry heaved before collapsing against the bowl. Her vision blurred as the pain coursed through her. She felt her stomach roll over but knew there was nothing left for her to empty from it. Her hands shook as they rested on the toilet bowl and her eyes watered.

The pain sat like a bolder on her chest making it hard to breathe and harder to move. She wanted nothing more that to curl up on the bathroom floor and never move again. But she couldn't bring herself to let go of the toilet bowl and it was the only thing holding her upright.

She felt the tears hit her hand before she even realized she was crying. She stared at the teardrop in disgust even as the sob bubbled out of her mouth.

"Goddamnit," she cursed, dragging her shaking hand over her mouth.

It took her three tries to flush the toilet and twice as many to get her feet under her again. Her legs shook but held steady despite the fact that her vision blurred. She grabbed the counter for support and leaned heavily against it.

Pain consumed her. Her stomach rolled. Her hands shook even as she clutched the counter to the point that her knuckles were white.

The reflection she saw in the mirror shocked her. The hollow-eyed, pale-faced girl staring back at her was not Darcy van Dyke. She closed her eyes for a moment hoping her vision would clear. She drew in a deep breath, fighting the pain that sat heavily in her chest.

She held the breath for a moment. If she could just get her heart to slow down she would be able to handle the rest. It was nothing a few Tylenols and some makeup couldn't fix. That's what she would tell herself. That's what she would keep telling herself in order to get through the day.

She turned on the tap and let the water run lukewarm. She washed the vomit off her hands, rinsed out her mouth, and splashed water in her face. She found the Tylenol she'd stashed in the cupboard above the sink and took four before brushing her teeth. She half-assed washed her hair in the sink and was towelling it off when someone knocked on the door.

"Just a second," she called out as she hung the towel back up and shook her hair out. She was reaching for her makeup bag when whoever was on the opposite side of the door knocked again.

"I said, just a second," she mumbled but couldn't bring herself to shout it. She tossed the bag on the counter. On unsteady legs she stepped towards the door, unlocked it, and pulled it open.

"There are other bathrooms," she began before she looked up and up to meet Drew's warm brown eyes.

He smiled sheepishly. "They're all occupied." He gave a half shrug, hands in the pockets of his jeans. He took in her pale face and tired eyes, but kept his concern masked. "Apparently this one is too. I'll just go."

"Nah, I'm done in here, Drew." She reached back to grab her makeup bag and stumbled. She would have ended up on the floor if he hadn't caught her arm.

"Steady now, Darcy."

His voice was deep and smooth with more south in it than there should have been for a man raised in Virginia. She took a moment to focus on that voice as her world spun and her vision tried to clear. When she was sure she had her legs under her again she offered him a shaky smile.

"I'll just grab my bag and get out of your hair." She picked up the bag and went to leave the bathroom but his hand was still on her arm.

"Darcy…" He let the concern fill that one word and waited for her bright blue eyes to meet his. "Are you alright?"

She offered him a smile and gave his hand a pat. "I'm just fine, Drew." She peeled his hand away and stepped around him. "I'll be back down in few minutes."

He watched her leave, her legs barely steady, and could feel the frown pull at his mouth. He knew that Anna wasn't all that happy with Darcy right now, but that was Anna's problem not his. They would work it out. And even though it wasn't his place, he knew he would talk to Alice about this the minute he got her alone. Because Darcy was family, that much had become clear to him pretty quick. And he'd always been raised to look out for family.

* * *

It took her a half hour before she felt ready to go back downstairs. The Tylenol had taken the edge off. The pain was just a heavy weight instead of a sharp throb. She was aware of it but she was pretty sure she'd be able to function. And today was all about being functional, about getting through.

She'd changed into clean clothes and spent more time than usual on her makeup. But still the sight of herself in the mirror shocked her. She was hollow eyed and pale faced. Her eyes were bloodshot from lack of sleep and vomiting. But she'd managed to hide most of the damage with mascara, foundation, and some eyeliner.

She checked her reflection once more before heading out of the room. Her hair had settled flat around her face, taking on a slight curl that reminded her of her mother's hair. She ran a hand through it, fingering the length. It had grown a bit since Evie had cut it all off, but it had a long way to go before it was anywhere near what it used to be. Still, she didn't mind the short hair. It was manageable.

The kitchen was quieter when she returned to it but she could hear the murmur of the TV from the living room. She could see Charlie with Mia in the living room, a kids program on the TV. Drew and Anna were nowhere in sight, likely enjoying the fact that they had a babysitter. Bea and Beth were at the sink doing dishes, completely in sync with one another. Duncan was behind his computer screen. Evie was making a list. And Alice was arguing with Coop.

Everyone was where they should be, Darcy thought as she took in the scene in front of her. She had a moment to feel out of place again. She felt, more often than not, that she didn't quite fit in with the McKnight family. Although she was always welcome, she didn't quite have a place. Everyone had a purpose, everyone had a place, and she was just Cooper's friend. The girl with no family to speak of that had to be doted on.

She closed her eyes for a moment at the bottom of the stairs. She needed to get her mind off the negative thoughts and back to the present. She needed to be happy today, or at least put on her best face. There would be too many people around for her to be miserable.

Coop watched her at the bottom of the stairs. He had no clue what Alice was saying anymore. His attention was fully on Darcy as she closed her eyes and collected herself. He'd been worried about her since she'd slipped away at breakfast but he knew better than to go after her. He would talk to her later about it, but he knew better than to try and find her when she was seeking solitude. It was best to wait for her to come to him.

He'd been pushy with her all throughout their high school years. He had demanded and he had interfered in her life. He had kidnapped her from her house and sheltered her as much as he could from the threat she faced. But he couldn't protect her from this. She had to deal with this on her own. And if she wanted to seek out his help, he knew that it would have to be on her own terms as well.

He noticed the makeup and wet hair. She had made an attempt to cover the lack of sleep and pain. But he could see it clearly. He wondered if she knew how openly she carried the pain. He doubted it. He guessed she thought she was putting on a good face, but he noticed every grimace, every tense muscle, and every scowl.

"Are you joinin' us, deary, or just standin' in the doorway all mornin'?" Evie didn't glance up from her list as she said the words but all eyes turned to her.

Darcy opened her eyes slowly and felt the smile tug at her lips. The woman had eyes in the back of her head. "Joining you," she confirmed moving into the kitchen and settling into a seat next to Coop.

She ignored his concerned glance and instead turned towards Evie. "What's the list for?"

Evie glanced over for half a second, long enough to take in the fatigue in the girl's eyes and fact that her voice was a little too cheerful. "Things I need to make sure to bring along to the big house this afternoon." She considered the list for another moment. "I think I've got everythin' now."

"We're heading over to the big house for the fireworks?" Darcy glanced over at Coop, her brow creased in confusion.

"Hey, I just found out too, darlin'. So don't go blaming me." He held up his hands.

"The whole clan's coming out for the party. Well, except Ruth and Erik who can't be bothered." Alice rolled her eyes.

"They did send a card though," Evie supplied, skimming over her list.

"Was there a big cheque in it?" Coop inquired and received a stern look from his mother.

"They said they regret being unable to attend." Evie set the pen down and looked over at the three of them. "John insisted we come to the big house so that's where we'll go. Any problems?"

Darcy shook her head. "I haven't been to the big house in ages. Nor have I seen the whole clan in a while."

"It'll definitely be a party," Coop commented glancing into his empty coffee mug and wondering where it had gone. "When does this shindig start?"

"Not until three-ish," Duncan mumbled from behind his laptop. He glanced up when all the eyes turned onto him. "Da said he didn't want a single soul on his property till after three."

"Well then." Coop grinned. "Looks like grandpa hasn't changed a bit."

"Did you expect him to?" Alice grabbed her mug and his to refill them. She raised a brow to Darcy who only nodded.

"I suppose not." He shrugged and glanced over as a chorus of giggles came from the living room. "She's really got a way with kids."

"That she does." Evie glanced over, a small smile on her lips. "Hopefully Mia isn't the only grandbaby around here for much longer." She sent Alice a meaningful look.

"Hey, enough of that." Alice waved her hand indicating all of what her mother had just said. "I don't have any time for that nonsense in my life right now."

"You're not getting any younger," Evie continued in the same nonchalant manner.

Alice glanced down at the coffee mugs she was filling and prayed for patience. "Thanks for the subtle reminder about my age, mum. Why don't you bother Beth or Bea about this and leave me be?"

"Beth is still in school and Bea is...well." Evie tore her list from the note pad and folded it in half. "I'm still hoping she'll bring a nice boy home, but mostly I would just like her to bring anyone home."

"I heard that," Bea stated from her place at the sink. She sent a grin over her shoulder at Darcy. "I'm off relationships at the moment, mum. So, you're out of luck."

"See, you're my only hope."

Alice groaned as she carried the mugs back to the table. "What about Coop? Why aren't you on his case?"

Evie looked over at her son as if considering and Coop tried to make himself as small as possible in his chair. "He's much too young."

"You were twenty-one when you married da," Alice countered as she sat down.

"Those were different times."

"So, that's how it's gonna be, eh?" Alice leaned back in her chair, her mug in her hands. "It's all on me."

Evie grinned, getting up from the table. "Yup, that's how it's gonna be."

Chapter 22

Coop let her hide out in the garage with him. It was not that he thought she needed to hide. Darcy had always been the most fearless person he knew. But he had seen the panic cross her face at the idea of going to the big house for Canada Day. And he figured that she needed a few hours of peace before they headed into the chaos.

He'd brought out a thermos of coffee that his mother had made up for them. She hadn't questioned them leaving. She rarely did. And then they had escaped the house to the sanctuary of the garage. The one place where they were both on equal grounds and where the world of problems always got put on hold.

Hours passed as they finished working on Dr. Dillon's truck and moved on to Miss Lorain's sedan. It needed an oil change and Cooper had an inkling that he would have to replace the wheel bearings. He'd taken it for a test drive and the steering wheel had almost shaken out of his hands once he'd passed sixty. It didn't really surprise him. Miss Lorain rarely went above forty any time she drove.

Darcy was sitting on his wheeled stool, spinning in circles absently. Her foot tapping along to the rock music pounding out of his stereo. She was watching him drain the oil from the sedan. She knew he wished they had a hoist in this garage, but they didn't spend enough time there to justify the renovation. So, he would do what he could without it and send Miss Lorain to the local guy for whatever else she needed done. She wouldn't like that, but he would make sure she was treated right.

He was cursing from his place underneath the sedan and it made her grin. It wasn't a day at the garage if someone wasn't swearing. She had picked up her bad language habits in her father's garage and so had Coop. But they had both learned to filter their words when it mattered most. In the garage there was no filter.

"Motherfucker!"

Coop slid out from underneath the sedan revealing a face half covered in oil. He wiped a hand across it and smeared the oil more.

"You know, you're supposed to drain that into the pan right?" She laughed.

He sent her a glare. "Keep that up and you'll have some of this on your face as well."

"You wouldn't dare." She hopped off the stool and passed him a clean rag.

He accepted it and attempted to clean off his face. "That'll take a few minutes to drain." He sat up on the crawler and tried to stretch out his sore back muscles. "God I miss my real garage."

He shoved the rag into the back pocket of his jeans as he got to his feet. "Any coffee left in that thing?"

She glanced back at the coffee urn. "We ran out like two hours ago, Coop. You complained about it two hours ago."

He ran a hand through his hair and sighed. "Shit." He went over to the mini fridge that was stashed in the corner. "We've got cola in here at least."

"I'll take one."

She caught it when he tossed it to her and drank deeply from the bottle. When she lowered it he was back beside her.

"So, you want to talk about it?"

She sent him a sideways glance as she took another sip from the cola. "No."

He nodded, grin still in place. "That's fine. I'll do the talking then I suppose." He caught her glare but wasn't put off by it. "I know it's not ideal in the least, having to go to the big house. I know we came here so you could have a quiet recovery. Hell, my family coming up for Canada Day was enough of a disruption not to add the whole McKnight clan into the mix. I'm just as ticked off as you should be about the whole thing. Given the choice, I would skip the whole deal and stay in this garage until everyone leaves."

"You'd get hungry pretty quick."

It was his turn to glare. "I'm being serious, Darcy."

"So am I." She set the bottle down and wandered away from him. "There's no food in here. After a few hours you'd be eating that rag in your pocket out of desperation."

"You're impossible."

She shrugged and ground her teeth against the wave of pain that ran through her. She really needed to stop doing that. "As if you didn't already know that."

"Darlin' I knew you were impossible the moment I met you and yet I still let you come over and play Sonic with me." He ran a hand through his hair again. "And kicked your ass at it."

Her eyes flared at that, as he knew they would. "Like hell you did."

"Sparky, you didn't know how to work a controller when I met you." He was getting her good and mad now, which always happened when he played on her competitive side.

"I can take you any day, McKnight."

He glanced at the wall clock and sighed. "Well, the epic gaming showdown will have to wait. It's time to head over to the big house."

She groaned and rubbed a hand over her face before remembering it would screw up her makeup. "Fuck."

He glanced over at her from hanging a tool back on the pegboard. "We gonna talk about it before we leave, or am I just supposed to pretend none of this is happening right now." He waved a hand to indicate all of her.

She bit her bottom lip and drew in a deep breath. "Fuck."

He resisted the urge to comment again. Instead, he waited as she paced back and forth, struggling with some internal dilemma.

"Goddamnit, Coop." She ran her hands through her hair sending it in all directions. "How am I supposed to put on a face for everyone? I can barely manage it for your family let alone the whole clan and half the town who will be at the big house!" She threw her hands up in the air. "Everyone will want to talk to me. Everyone will want to ask about the accident." She met his gaze, her bottom lip trembling slightly. "I can't do that."

He crossed to her and laid a hand gently on her left shoulder, avoiding the burnt area. He used his other hand to lift her face to meet his gaze. "The minute you don't want to be there we'll leave."

She raised a brow. "They're your family. I can't let you do that."

"Since when d'you let me do anything?"

She lowered her head to his chest and sighed. "I can't keep taking you away from them, Coop." Her hand found his where it was still resting lightly against her face. She linked her fingers with his. "I won't be blamed for you missing anything again."

He took a step back and once again forced her to meet his gaze. "No one blames you for anything, Darcy."

She bit her lip, her emotions a storm at the moment. Grief, anger, and pain mixed together making her want to cry.

She hated herself for wanting to cry for the second time today. She hated not being able to get a handle on what was going on in her life. And she hated seeing the concern in Cooper's eyes.

"Even if they don't, they should," she grumbled leaning her head back against his chest because she couldn't bring herself to look him in the eye any longer. "I take you away from them."

"And I have no choice in the matter?"

She caught the hint of anger in his voice and glanced up. The concern was gone now. She'd hit a nerve. She could tell by the way his eyes narrowed. "I didn't mean it like that."

"We both made our choices, Darcy. So, don't go playin' the martyr on this. I wanted to leave Senoia as much as you when high school ended. We left together but we both had our reasons."

She nodded because she didn't trust herself to speak just yet. She knew he was right. She knew that she was just riding the emotional turmoil and not thinking straight. But it had been a long time since he'd talked to her like that. A long time since he'd firmly put her in her place during an argument and she was taking a moment to process it.

"Now, do we have more to hash out before we deal with my family or can we go?"

"I'm sorry," she mumbled and watched the grin spread across his face.

"No you aren't, darlin'." He ruffled her already messy hair. "You said what you wanted to say, as you always do."

He glanced around the garage and knew that once again he wouldn't get around to picking up after himself. Andy would have disapproved, but he found he cared less and less for what Andy would have approved of as time went on.

"C'mon, we've got a party to get to." He took her hand and pulled her towards the door.

"Don't we have to help the others?" She glanced up at the house. "Don't we have to bring something?"

"We already talked about this, Sparky." He flashed her a winning smile. "How the hell are we supposed to carry lobsters on the bike?"

* * *

Anna watched the Honda tear out of the driveway, a frown on her face. "And there they go again. Leaving without helping at all."

Evie glanced over from where she was working on a bowl of potato salad at the counter. Mia was on the floor at her feet, content to colour in the old colouring book they'd dug out. Evie gave the little one a smile before turning her attention back to her own daughter.

"What's crawled up your butt and died lately?" she asked, her voice cheerful but the question direct.

Anna jolted at the question and turned to her mother. "Pardon?"

"You've been as ornery as a gator with a toothache since ya got here." She watched the younger woman open her mouth to protest but held up a hand. "Now, not openly and not with your sisters, but you've been givin' poor Darcy the sink eye since you walked through the door. So, what the Devil is goin' on?"

"Poor Darcy," Anna mumbled crossing her arms and hitching her hip up onto the kitchen table. "It's always poor Darcy this and poor Darcy that. She's always here and she's always being doted on as though she's a lost little bird with a broken wing."

"I didn't raise you to be this bitter woman I see right now, Annabelle," Evie's voice was stern and her hands were placed firmly on her hips.

"She just takes and takes. Just showed up one day and never left. Now we're all supposed to just accept her as part of the family, but what does she give back?"

"Annabelle Jean Louise McKnight." Evie raised her voice slightly, but she was mindful of the child at her feet. She didn't need to frighten Mia or draw the attention of the rest of the family that was still scattered throughout the house. "What has Darcy ever done to you?"

"She took Cooper away. After all we've done for her, she took him." Anna knew she sounded childish saying it but the memory was still a barb in her side. "On the one day I really needed him, she had him."

"Lord Almighty I ought to knock some sense into ya, girl." Evie closed her eyes and prayed for strength. She bent to pick up Mia so that she would have something to do with her hands, because at the moment she was feeling mildly violent. "Cooper made his own choices. He's a grown man, or about grown anyhow, and he chose to be with his best friend when she needed him."

"Rather than his sister?" Anna pouted. She felt dumb, but she needed to hash this out. Her mother wouldn't let her walk away from it now.

"It was your wedding, but it was her mama's funeral." Evie drew a deep breath at the wave of emotion that ran over her. "I missed my best friend's funeral to see you walk down the aisle because that boneheaded husband of hers wouldn't change the date. Cooper made his choice to be with Darcy. And if you can't be an adult about that and let it go, I didn't raise ya right like I thought."

Feeling thoroughly chastised Anna reached for her daughter and placed Mia on her hip. She had no clue why she was pushing this or why it mattered so much right now. The emotions just seemed to bubble up inside her and spill out. She pressed a kiss to Mia's curly hair and took a moment to gather her thoughts.

"Why'd ya ever take her in, mama?"

Evie raised a brow at the question. She'd thought the answer had always been clear to her children, but perhaps she had been wrong. "Liv was my best friend and your da and I are Darcy's Godparents. It's no matter that's she grown now. She ain't got no one else."

"She's practically lived with us since we moved to Senoia."

"And we've been blessed with enough to have her here," Evie snapped. "You need to cleanse that bitterness from your heart Annabelle before it turns the whole thing black."

Anna opened her mouth to respond but found no words. She closed it firmly and settled for looking at the floor.

"That girl has been through more than you could imagine." Evie raised a brow in consideration. "Though I suppose you could imagine given your job." She let that statement hang in the air for a moment and waited for her daughter's gaze to meet hers again. "And now she's been through another ordeal and she's just trying to get better. This," Evie waved a hand at her, "isn't helping her do that."

"What am I supposed to do?" Anna mumbled, cuddling her daughter close. She hadn't felt this small since she'd been a teenager, caught sneaking out of the house.

"Get to know the girl and stop being such a stick in the mud." Evie turned back to the counter to sprinkle paprika on top of her salad. She gave a satisfied nod before turning back to her daughter.

"But right now you can get everyone rounded up and get this food loaded. We've gotta head over now."

"Yes, mum." Anna nodded.

Evie watched her leave the kitchen, toddler on her hip, and wondered where the hell all of that had even come from and how long it had been festering there. She'd always believed it was best to deal with a problem the minute it happened. But if Anna had been mad at Darcy since the wedding she'd been sitting on that bitterness for a few years.

She blew out a breath. How had she not noticed? The answer was pretty simple. Coop and Darcy hadn't been around for many family events for the last few years. Racing had taken them away. When they did make it home, it wasn't when everyone else was around. So, she hadn't been faced with Anna's monster.

Alice had mentioned it but Evie hadn't wanted to believe it. She hadn't wanted to think about Anna being that petty. But part of her understood. The part that knew how it felt to be jaded and replaced. Evie had always tried to love her children equally, to give them whatever they needed. She hoped that she had done her job. But now she wondered and she didn't like how that made her feel, not one bit.

Chapter 23

F*ifteen Years Ago...*

She felt the anticipation build up inside her as the sky gradually transitioned into dusk. The band on stage continued to play and people milled about, but she sat still in her sundress and waited.

Her mama and dad sat behind her in lawn chairs. They got to sit in lawn chairs because they were grown ups. She had to sit on the grass because she was a kid. She didn't mind so much. And soon Coop would be there with her and she would get to see the fireworks.

She tapped her foot in anticipation. Behind her mama was talking about something with her dad. They were laughing. It was nice to see them laughing and having a good time. They both worked too much. They were too busy. They never laughed. But they were holding hands now. They were laughing. And mama looked happy. Her smile was big and her sundress was bright blue. She even wore the floppy hat that Darcy had picked out for her.

Darcy looped her hands around her knees and pulled them closer to her chest. She was so excited. They had never taken her to the fireworks before. They had always left her at home with the babysitter. Sure, she could see them out the window but it wasn't the same as being there.

She had been worried that she would get tired before they had a chance to go off. But she couldn't imagine being tired now. Energy raced through her. She couldn't keep her feet still though she tried because mama had told her to sit still and behave. And she wanted to be a good girl. She didn't want to ruin the night when mama was having such a good time.

She heard them before she saw them. The McKnight family was not a quiet bunch mostly because of the number of them. She wanted to get to her feet and run to them but she stayed where she was. She would be good today.

Coop ran over and came to a sliding stop beside her. He nearly tumbled on top of her but he regained his balance in time. He was a gangly mess even at seven. Too thin and mostly arms and legs, but she was still taller than him, much to his displeasure. Mostly because she never let him forget it.

He sat down on the grass beside her and grinned. He was missing some teeth, but his smile was genuine. "Sorry I'm late. Annie took forever!"

Darcy glanced back at his second oldest sister who was dressed in a white mini skirt and red and blue top. She looked rather patriotic, Darcy thought. Her long brown hair was curled and fell in waves over her shoulders. She was chatting with a few of her friends and giggling over something.

"Silly girls needing to look just right." Coop rolled his eyes then slid a glance her way wondering if she would get offended.

"I'll never understand." She shrugged returning his grin.

She watched Miss Evelyn greet her mama with a kiss on the cheek and give her dad a hug. Coop's dad waved as he set up lawn chairs but didn't move over to say hello. She had always liked Mr. McKnight. He told good jokes and he always had gummies in his office. But he was not one for big crowds her mama had once said and she could tell he looked a bit out of place right now. She felt bad for him.

"Why did your dad come if he doesn't want to be here?"

Coop gave her a strange look before glancing back at his father. He hadn't thought it was that obvious. "To make mum happy."

Darcy accepted that answer and turned her attention back towards the sky. "They're gonna start soon."

He glanced over at her. He'd never seen her this wound up about anything before. She was practically vibrating with excitement. "When the band plays the anthem that's when they'll go off."

She glanced over at him, blue eyes wide. "Really?"

He grinned and slung an arm around her shoulders companionably. "Just wait, you'll see."

* * *

Present Day...

The big house was just that, a big house. It had been a simple two-bedroom farmhouse at one point in time but over the years additions had been added to it to accommodate the ever-growing McKnight clan.

Duncan was the second youngest of five children and as he told it, the first addition had been there when he was born. The second had been put up when his younger sister had come along and the family of four boys had needed to make room for another girl in the house besides their mama.

Darcy had always liked the big house. It just shouted family to her. There were memories in that house. There were generations of stories in those walls. And a person could see that just by looking at the exterior. Never mind what you encountered when you went inside. It was covered in pictures, trophies, articles, and memorabilia for every member of the family. John and Maureen McKnight were nothing if not sentimental.

The yard was already crowded when they pulled up on the bike. People were setting up tables and laying out food.

Jimmy and Malcolm, the oldest of Duncan's siblings, were arguing at the grill and there were children running about.

Coop killed the engine and swung off the bike. He knew Darcy would take a moment before she got off. He knew she was in pain. He could tell by the vice grip she'd had around him the whole ride, but he'd remembered to pack the Tylenol and her meds if she got desperate enough to take them. He didn't think she would but he could hope.

"It looks like we're late." Darcy set the helmet on the seat in front of her and scanned the yard in front of her.

Coop glanced at the clock on his display. "We're right on time. Everyone else is early."

"Figures." She rolled her eyes and swung off the bike. The world spun and she was glad Coop was there to grab her by the elbows and stop her from falling over.

"None of that today," he murmured in her ear and waited for her to be steady before releasing her. "Leave the staggering to the professionals today."

She ground her teeth together, riding out the wave of pain then stepped away from his grip. "I think I'm good."

"Counting on it, darlin'." He grinned. "Now, let's go see who we can distract long enough to avoid doing any work at all."

"We have to help out," she protested.

"You are here to recover," his voice was stern and at war with the laughter in his eyes. "So, we're gonna make the most of this."

"You just want to avoid doing any heavy lifting," she grumbled.

"Damn right I do. And if I need to exploit you a little bit to do it I'm not above doing that." He linked an arm with her and began walking towards the yard.

"You're a scoundrel, Cooper McKnight."

"You wouldn't have it any other way," he countered and had her laughing. He knew that if she was laughing she might not be thinking of how much pain she was in.

They had barely made it a couple feet before the football came flying towards them. Coop had just enough time to grab it before it slammed into his face and he blinked in surprise. He looked around him and found the culprit immediately.

"Still got quick reflexes." Andrea Houtkooper, or Andy to anyone who knew her for more than half a second, grinned as she walked over to them. Her ginger hair was tucked into an Irwin ball cap and her athletic, 5'6" build was clad in jean shorts and a tank top. "You gonna join us for a game later?"

"You convince the usual characters and I'm in." Cooper eyed his cousin who he hadn't seen in at least two years. "Ya look good, Andy."

"You don't look half terrible either, Coop." Her gaze slid over to Darcy and her grin broadened. "Glad you're not dead, but I suppose you'll be sittin' out this game."

Darcy chuckled. She couldn't help it. Andy was as blunt as they came and she meant no harm by it. "Yeah, I think I'll join the cheerleaders this year."

"Damn shame. We could have used a decent runner." Andy glanced at Coop. "I suppose you'll have to do." She plucked the football from his hands before he could retort. "I'll catch up with ya'll later. I need to convince everyone else now."

Darcy watched her jog off and could only shake her head. "Well, she hasn't changed."

Coop ran a hand through his hair and watched his cousin corner someone else to strong-arm him into a game of touch football. "No, she hasn't." He glanced over at her. "I'm not that slow, am I?"

She gave him a sympathetic smile and patted his arm. "No, Coop. But molasses in January is speedy in comparison."

She watched his eyes widen and knew she'd gotten him.

"Oh, you'll pay for that one." He went to grab her but she spun away.

"You'll have to catch me first," she laughed and, ignoring all advisories, ran away from him. And God it felt good to run again. She knew she would pay for it later, but right now she was laughing and running. Right now, she was having fun. Right now, she felt alive.

Chapter 24

John Douglas McKnight hadn't planned on hosting a massive shindig for Canada Day. In fact, it had all been rather last minute. Usually, he would just sit on the porch with his wife and watch the fireworks like any other year. But after Maureen's stroke in the spring she had been adamant that they do the big gathering.

He would grumble about it to her face, but it was nice to have the whole family together. Especially since he didn't know how much longer Maureen would be with him to celebrate things. He was an optimistic man, but he wasn't naïve. He'd served in a war after all; death was just something that happened. He wasn't insensitive to it. He just knew how the world worked.

He glanced out at his wife, her white hair freshly done from the salon in town just for today. She had a smile on her face as she sat at the picnic table with his oldest boys. Likely bugging them for their lack of spouse or their long beards. It didn't matter that his beard was just as long, she would always bother them about theirs.

He liked seeing her smiling and laughing with her kids. He hated looking out at her and thinking that one-day she wouldn't be there. He tried to keep those thoughts at the back of his mind but every now and then they would creep forward. Usually at times like this, when she was happy. Times when he wanted to remember her the most.

He'd always thought he would be the first one to go. He'd thought the war would take him but he'd made it through that with minimum damage. Then he'd thought the sea would take him. But he'd retired from fishing a few years ago and was still no worse for wear. He went out with his boys every now and then but his old bones couldn't take it. He knew that much. And although he was more stubborn than most, he knew his limitations.

So instead he was watching his wife slip away from him. Something he had never thought would happen. Maureen, his rock, his safe haven. She was his world and had been for sixty years. He just hoped the doctor was right in saying she would be around for a few more years now as long as she took it easy. She didn't seem so confident, but she'd always been skeptical about medicine. He just needed to convince her to take it easy. That was the hard part.

"Da?"

John turned from the window, the voice snapping him out of his train of thought. His youngest son was standing in the doorway of the living room, his hands deep in his pockets and a curious expression on his face.

"Going deaf in your old age, pops?" Duncan smiled and crossed to the room to give his father a hug. "I've been calling you for a good five minutes."

"Huh," John muttered returning the hug. "Was off in my own little world."

"Clearly." Duncan stepped out of the hug and gave his father a once over. The man had looked the same for as long as he could remember. Sure, his hair had gotten a little whiter and his face was a little more lined but very little had changed about the man's appearance. He was still a burly man, built by the military and tested by the sea. Age had softened him a little, but barely. He was still someone you wouldn't want to mess with.

Duncan had never really fit in with his family. If he were put in a line up with them the only thing he'd have in common would be his height and his hazel eyes. Otherwise, he looked like the high school geek that fell in with the football team. The thought put a smile on his face.

"Why you hiding in the house when everyone else is outside?"

John glanced around the living room trying to remember what he'd come in for. "Maureen sent me in for somethin'. Don't know what it was now."

Duncan, having already spoken to his mother outside, knew that he'd been sent in to get more ice. But he wasn't about to correct the man. "Well, I'm on a mission for ice. Want to help me carry it out? About everyone is here now."

John ran a hand over his beard and nodded. He followed his son into the kitchen and considered him for a moment. The boy hadn't gone into the family business like his brothers and he hadn't done anything physical like his sister. No, he sat at a computer all day. John had never quite been able to wrap his mind around it, but the boy was smart. He'd always known that.

"The whole bloody town turned out for this damn thing," John muttered. "I should have known when Maureen said she told the church we were having a party."

"She told the church?" Duncan sent him a sympathetic glance. He'd been on the receiving end of those social strategies before.

"Well, there's no stopping her when she sets her mind to something," he grumbled as he dug out a bag of ice and passed it to Duncan. "I had suggested we have the family by and she seemed to think all of Chester counts as family."

"Well, ya'll have been part of this community for a long time, Da."

"Bugger off." He sent his son a narrow-eyed look. "Whose side are you on anyways?"

"Mum's, always." He grinned taking the second bag of ice from him. "The woman is terrifying."

John chuckled, a deep warm sound that brought Duncan back to his childhood. "You're right on that one." He sent a sideways glance at his son. "You got yourself quite a firecracker too."

Duncan smiled as they moved towards the door. "Evie's a force to be reckoned with. We've had our fair share of standoffs, but none that left us too worse for wear. She's a hell of a woman and a hell of a mother."

"I always liked her, for a southerner."

Duncan chuckled. "You never did hold that against her."

"Well, she could drink like a sailor when ya met her and still make it to church on Sunday. And any woman who can do that is good in my books." He glanced across the lawn towards his wife as they stepped outside. "She reminded me a lot of your mother if I'm being completely honest."

Duncan smiled and would have slung an arm around his father's shoulders had his hands not been full of ice. "Formidable women, every man should be so lucky."

"You're damn right."

* * *

Darcy watched them come out of the house and couldn't help but think she'd never seen two men so different in her life. Duncan, his arms full of ice, looked so far from a fisherman's son that it was jarring, yet he was in an easy conversation with his father. Smiles were on both of their faces and their laughter drifted down to her.

It reminded her again why she loved this family. They embraced their differences. Rather than strong-arming a reluctant child into the family trade, they encourage the pursuit of dreams, no matter how farfetched. The McKnights had always been dreamers. Sure more than half of them were fisherman, but not because they had to be but because they chose to be.

She glanced over at Coop who was wrestling a toddler in the grass. His second cousin Joshua was barely school age and a ball of energy. The older sibling, Madison, was kicking a soccer ball around with Charlie.

She wondered what it would have been like if Duncan had made Coop study computer science. If he had forced him to take over the family legacy or some such nonsense. The idea amused her as much as it made her sad. She could never see him happy behind a desk. She could never see him happy anywhere but elbow deep in an engine.

She watched him toss Joshua over his shoulder and cart him across the yard towards his father, Quinn, and deposit the young boy on his lap. There was a torrent of giggles, some squirming, and then the boy was running off to join his sister with the soccer ball.

Darcy grinned from her place on the grass. She was staying away from the chaos as much as possible, Coop thought as he met her gaze. His family was running around with plates of food and full drink cups. The whole town was there too or would be before nightfall. He knew that the fire department, mostly because he'd talked to his Aunt Louise, who was a member, would be there shortly to start setting up the display down by the water. His grandfather had enough property that it would be far enough away from everyone. It really was the perfect spot for it.

He'd left Darcy to sit in the grass. He knew that she needed the time to herself. He knew that she was in pain and that the people weren't doing her any good. So, the best he could do was run interference. He mingled. He chatted. He caught up with family. He did what he was supposed to do.

Playing with Joshua had been pure indulgence. Other than Mia, there were no kids in his family yet. It was only at larger events like this that he saw his second cousins and it always brought a smile to his face. There was no one so full of life like a toddler. Hell, anyone under ten would wear him into the ground. And he was willing to let it happen.

He wandered over to join her on the grass, dropping down and stretching his long legs out in front of him. He crossed them at the ankle, his work boots looking beaten and scuffed, and leaned back on his elbows. The weather was warm, but the breeze from the water counteracted it nicely. It would be a clear night, he judged by the sky, and if the wind stayed the same it would be almost perfect.

"You lost in dreamland, McKnight?"

He cast a sideways glance her way before looking back up at the sky. "Nah, just enjoying being out here. It's been too damn long since I've sat on the grass and just enjoyed the ocean breeze while my family causes chaos."

She felt the immediate pang of guilt and struggled to push it aside. "It is nice to be here. I've always liked this place." She laughed as she watched Joshua steal the ball from his sister and do a victory dance. "And your family's alright."

"They'll do in a pinch." He smiled watching them interact much as she was. "They're all glad that you're alright," he said it causally but he watched her stiffen. "They're just waiting for you to actually come join the festivities."

She shifted on the grass. She'd abandoned her jacket for comfort and because the sun was making her sweat, but she'd been careful to keep herself turned away from the crowd. She didn't want to talk to people about her accident. She didn't want to show off her burns to his family any more than she'd wanted to at Dave's Place to the townsfolk.

She cast a glance at her jacket and knew that if she attempted to put it back on the pain would do her in. She'd hit a neutral place with the pain she was in. It was there. She was aware of it. But as long as she didn't do anything to aggravate it she thought she could handle it. She hoped she could handle it.

She looked over at Coop and found him watching her expectantly. "Can't I just stay here and be anti-social?"

"Darlin', you can do whatever you want. But they'll come find you eventually." He pushed to his feet and looked down at her. "You might as well face them on even ground."

"You don't play fair, Coop."

He extended a hand to her. "You'd be confused if I started now."

She took his hand with a smile. No, she couldn't picture him anyway other than how he was.

Chapter 25

They sat around the bon fire waiting for dusk to settle into darkness. The children had settled down, completely full of marshmallows and candy. Everyone else had eaten their fill of lobster, burgers, fish, deserts, and numerous salads. Darcy had lost track of the number of items of food that had been pushed at her all day. She had avoided most of it, but she had been forced to eat a few bites here and there.

She'd spoken to townsfolk. She'd seen the Clooney sisters and Mr. O'Hare and rehashed their encounter at Dave's Place. She'd run into Dr. Dillon and his family where Coop sassed him about his automotive maintenance habits. And she'd had a chance to thank Susan from the bakery for the great cake that Bea had brought her.

She'd talked with Coop's family. She'd joked with his uncles about fishing and teased his cousin Chris about his new military haircut. She'd tugged on beards, kissed cheeks, and avoided hugs.

The only person she hadn't talked to was Louise. Being a firefighter, Darcy knew that Louise was less ignorant to her issues than the rest of them. So, she had sidestepped that encounter for most of the day. Still, she'd noticed the older woman's eyes following her, a shadow of understanding in them that she wasn't entirely comfortable with.

Darcy had scored the game of touch football that had turned into a game of tackle football. Charlie had whined about them not playing soccer. But precedent had won out seeing as she could single handedly beat a team of five of them, which she had proven two years ago.

Coop, despite his opposition to playing regulated sports in school, was a good athlete. She watched in envy as they all ran in the field across the street. She wanted nothing more than to join in on the fun but the heavy weight of the pain was a reminder of why she was scoring the game and not playing.

Alice had checked up on her a few times. Evie had sat with her for a bit and made her eat some salad. And she had caught concerned glances all day. But she was still doing fine. She was still holding her own.

Her bottle of Tylenol was almost empty but she didn't want to think about that. She didn't want to acknowledge how many she'd actually taken today, especially when they hadn't really touched the pain she was in. She wanted nothing more than to take one of her real pills, curl up in a ball, and sleep. But that wasn't an option right now. She just needed to make it through today.

She sat by the fire, one of three that had been made on the property. The air was cooling nicely with the evening and she was grateful for the warmth, but she didn't want to think of the source. She couldn't bring herself to look at the flames. She tried to focus on the conversation that was going on between Jimmy and Malcolm, Coop's oldest uncles.

"If you had listened to me, we wouldn't have lost a whole net of fish." Jimmy threw his hands up theatrically.

Malcolm grinned. "If you hadn't been drunker than a skunk, I wouldn't have ignored ya."

They'd told this story before. She could tell by the way they both took on the roles for it and she had to appreciate the way they played it up for the audience. Mia was giggling and clapping from her place on Anna's lap. Her eyes heavy with sleep, but not yet ready for bed. Drew sat with his arm around his wife's shoulders and a beer dangling loosely between his fingers. She knew that he'd been nursing the same beer all day. She could respect that.

"So, Louise and the gang have got it all set up at the shore." Gerald, the third oldest, joined them at the fire sitting next to his wife Tammy. "Looks like we'll be ready to go in about a half hour."

"About damn time." Jimmy toasted with his beer and downed what was left in it before adding it to the pile of empties. He opened another and took a pull from the bottle. "Did ya tell Da?"

"Before I came over here." Gerald ignored the skeptical note in his tone. "This ain't my first rodeo, Jimbo."

Jimmy started to say something crass, but glanced at the children present and thought better of it.

"Saved by little ears." Gerald smiled and sent a wink at Mia who broke out in a new round of giggles. He glanced over at Alice, who was seated with Coop and Darcy. "When are you gonna give us some little ones, Ali-cat?"

Alice dropped her head in her hands and wished for something stronger than her beer. "Is there something in the water or did ya'll just agree to bother me about this today?"

He held up his hands in surrender. "Just curious is all. It's not like we've got a great track record in this family anyhow when it comes to the oldest siblings."

"Hey!" Jimmy gave him a narrow-eyed look across the fire.

"Tell me I'm wrong. You're a forever bachelor and Malcolm is divorced with two kids he hasn't seen since they were in diapers." He took a sip of his beer. "Least Louise and I have two kids each." He gave his wife a kiss on the cheek. "And Duncan somehow managed six."

"Well, don't expect me to carry on that torch." Alice downed her beer and tossed it with the empties. "No way in hell."

"Count me out too." Coop looked terrified at the idea.

Darcy laughed, elbowing him in the ribs. "Awe c'mon, Coop. You could have a whole troop of rug-rats runnin' around."

"And who exactly would the lucky woman be?" Coop raised a brow. "They're not exactly lining up for the job."

"You're not exactly trying," she countered. It was an old argument between them, but there was something in the way he looked at her just then that wasn't quite the same.

"I guess I just figure the right one will come along eventually. So, why waste my time on just anybody?"

"For the fun of it?" Jimmy, who had always been able to find a willing woman when he wanted one, counselled. "Life's too short to just wait around."

"How about you, Darcy?" Gerald sent her a wink and earned a pinch from his wife. "Still avoiding capture."

"I live life in the fast lane. I'd have to find a fellow who could keep up first."

"And a guy who can put up with you," Anna muttered from her place across the fire.

"Pardon?" Darcy glanced over at her, finally bringing her gaze to the flames for the first time that evening. She felt the jolt the minute her eyes were drawn to them, felt the panic rise up but tried to focus on Anna.

"You heard me." Anna bounced Mia on her knee, not noticing that all of the eyes had turned to her. "I have never met someone so whiny, self-absorbed, and self-important. And I've met a lot of really terrible people. You're a complete leech on the family. You take up all of Cooper's time and now he's never home. You just take, take, take and give absolutely nothing back. You greedy, needy, little –"

"Annabelle!" Coop found his voice and although he only raised it enough to cut through her rant the anger in it set Mia off crying. He felt bad about that, in the back of his mind, but he would deal with that later.

Her eyes met his, never in her life had she seen so much anger in those brown orbs. Cooper, who was always calm and relaxed, looked as though he would strangle her if she said another word. She opened her mouth to do something, say something, but she never got that far.

Darcy, finally finding that she could move her legs, which had been frozen in shock, shot to her feet. She stumbled over the bench she'd been sitting on and managed to make it half a step before face planting. She pushed herself up, swallowing the wave of nausea brought on by the pain of ramming into the ground. She was on her feet and running before anyone could move. She needed to get away from there, from them.

Coop took a moment to send Anna a hate-filled glare, just half a second really, before he was on his feet and chasing after her.

The group around the fire exchanged glances, but no one said anything. There were some things that even they knew were off limits. Some things just had to run their own course.

Alice looked at her sister for a moment while everyone else sat silently. She thought about Anna's recent rant along with her behaviour over the last day. After a moment, the smile spread across her face. "You're pregnant."

"What!?" Anna's eyes found Alice's across the fire. She was still trying to process what she'd said, what she'd done, all while trying to calm Mia down. "No, I'm not."

"Yeah, you are," Alice said triumphantly.

"Told you so." Drew grinned taking a whimpering Mia from her so that she could get up and pace.

"No, I can't be pregnant." Anna threw her hands up. "I just had my…" She calculated in her head, muttered a curse, and sat back down. "How the hell did you know?"

"You haven't been this much of a –"

"Crusty windbag?" Drew supplied before Alice could use more colourful language.

"Thank you." She sent him a grateful smile. "You haven't been this much of a crusty windbag since last time you were pregnant."

Anna scowled. "Well…fudge."

Chapter 26

Darcy raced across the lawn. She knew someone was following her but she couldn't afford to slow down or stop. The pain all but blinded her. Her stomach rolled and she clamped her teeth down against the nausea. She could barely breathe and her lungs screamed at her as she continued to run.

She fumbled with the doorknob. Her hands were shaking, but on the third try she got it open and stumbled into the kitchen. She didn't know the big house as well as she knew the McKnight's place, but she knew where the bathroom was.

Darcy closed the door and leaned against it. She didn't care that it put pressure on her burns. She ignored the shocks that radiated across her shoulders and up her neck. She just needed a minute, she thought as she closed her eyes and drew in a deep breath. Just a minute and then she would be fine.

The bathroom light was brighter than she remembered and she kept her eyes closed against it. She focused on her breathing as the nausea continued to hit her in waves. Her lungs stopped screaming for air, but her heart still raced and her hands still shook.

"Fuck," she muttered as she felt her knees give out and she slid down the door. She ground her teeth together against the pain, whimpering as she rode it out until she was firmly on the floor.

"Well, looks like I'm staying here."

Darcy glanced around the bathroom through narrowed eyes. It was a small powder room with barely enough space to hold two people. She knew the main bathroom was upstairs and there was another in one of the additions. But this was where she was.

She drew in a shaky breath as the pain coursed through her, making her stomach roll. Her eyes fell on the toilet, which was at least a foot and a half away. She wasn't certain if she could make that if she tried. She glanced at the much closer wastebasket by the sink. She grabbed it, removed the bag, and held the plastic bin against her.

She leaned forward, testing whether she could get to her feet again, and her head spun. She felt the bile rise up in her throat and quickly leaned back against the door. She swallowed hard, letting her head thump back against the wood. Nope, she thought, fuck no.

"I'll just stay right here." She rubbed a hand across her face, which was now flushed and warm. Her hands shook as she clasped them together around the wastebasket.

What the hell had that been all about? She wondered staring into the bottom of the wastebasket as if it held the answers. She'd never had anyone in Coop's family address her with such hate. She'd never had anyone, with the exception of her father, say such things to her.

She blinked back the tears that threatened to come, partially from the pain and partially from the memories. She bit her lip as it trembled and let out a sob. She didn't realize the tears were falling until they hit the wastebasket in front of her.

"What did I ever do to her?" Darcy sobbed rocking slightly as she held the basket. The movement was what did her in. Moments later she lost everything she'd eaten that evening into the basket.

She groaned as she set it aside and wiped the back of her hand across her mouth. She felt a little better. At least the nausea was gone. But the pain was still enough that her mind could barely function and her vision blurred at the edges.

The knocking at the door had her closing her eyes again and praying she could disappear.

"Darlin', let me in."

She heard Coop's voice and felt the smile tug at her lips. At least it had been him who had come after her. Then again, of course it had been him. He would always come after her, she told herself.

"Just let me die in peace, Coop," she replied, her voice shaky. She hated that she could hear the tears in it.

"No can do." He turned the knob and was glad to find it unlocked. "If you're against this door I suggest you move."

"No can do," she parroted letting her eyes close. She felt the exhaustion set in. She'd passed the 36-hour mark long ago. She kept her eyes closed even as Coop slowly pushed the door open, moving her across the floor. She gritted her teeth against the fresh wave of pain from the pressure on her back.

"Sorry, darlin'." He slipped through the doorway when it was opened wide enough and crouched down beside her. "If you'd have moved..."

He trailed off when he got his first clear look at her face. The makeup she'd put on earlier in the day now ran down her pale face showing the tracks of her tears. She clutched the wastebasket, still rocking slightly, and her hands shook. Her eyes were closed and he could see that her jaw was clenched as she rode out the pain she was in.

He'd seen her look worse. He knew that. He tried to remember that as his hands balled into fists and the anger rolled through him. Anna was lucky their mum had raised him not to hit girls, because he'd been close to decking her for what she'd said. And looking at Darcy now, the urge was just as strong. He'd seen her worse, but he'd never seen her like this.

He drew in a deep breath and let it out slowly, trying to steady himself.

"You gonna throw up again, darlin'?" He watched her shake her head and gently pulled the wastebasket from her hands. He set it aside, telling himself he'd deal with it later. "Can you open your eyes?"

She shook her head again and felt the nausea rise back up. She needed to stop doing that.

Coop ran a hand through his hair. He didn't want to touch her. His hands were balled into fists again and they weren't quite steady. She was crying again. She was rocking and crying silently in the middle of the bathroom floor and there was nothing that he could do about it. He would do anything for her but there was nothing he could do right now. Nothing he could think to do.

"Tell me what to do, darlin'." He reached over and ran a hand over her hair. Her eyes fluttered open at the contact. "I'm at my wits end here."

"Just give me the pills and let me disappear." Her voice was shallow and barely a whisper, but it was filled with pain and sadness. "I'm a waste of space anyhow."

The hand that was stroking her hair tightened into a fist and he brought it to his mouth, tapping it against his lips. "I'm going to kill Anna."

"She's right." Darcy let her eyes drift closed again as the pain consumed her. She tugged her knees to her chest and rested her head on them. "I'm just taking up everyone's time and space. It would be better if I was gone."

"Don't talk like that."

"Just leave me the damn pills, Coop. And leave me alone."

She sounded defeated. That was all he could think as he looked at her sitting there. Worse than that, she looked completely defeated. He'd never in his life seen her back down from anything. And now she was all but asking him to leave her there to die. He wasn't going to do that any more than he would have left her in the fire.

The pills were in his pocket. They'd been there all day along with the Tylenol that she'd been downing like it was candy. He knew she hadn't slept. He knew that she'd thrown up all that she'd eaten that evening. She was hurting physically, that much was obvious, but what Anna had said had gotten to her more than he would bet even Anna had expected it would. Then again, Anna didn't know what she'd been through.

"No can do, darlin'." He got to his feet and stepped over her to the sink. Like always, his grandma kept paper cups beside it. He filled one and joined her on the floor. "I'm gonna give you one pill." He set the cup down as he dug out the bottle and shook one out.

"I want you to take this." He pressed the pill to her lips until she opened her mouth. "And slowly drink the water."

She wanted to protest, but the thought of the painkiller was too appealing. And the water was like ice soothing her sore throat. She sipped it slowly, swallowing the pill, and drinking the rest of the cup down as he held it to her lips. She drew in a deep breath when he pulled it away and already felt slightly better.

His hands were steady but he wasn't. He knew that he needed to keep it together for her right now. He needed to get her out of the bathroom and home to bed. But he wasn't certain how he was going to manage that. Mostly, he just wanted to get her to open her eyes and look at him. He wanted her to know that he was there.

He refilled the water and held it to her lips again. She took a sip but shook her head. Setting it aside, he leaned back against the vanity, his long legs brushing up against hers. There was no room to move with the two of them on the bathroom floor, but moving wasn't a priority at the moment.

"Feeling any better?" He knew it was a useless question but he asked it anyway, if only to fill the silence.

"Mmhm." She could feel him watching her and tried to open her eyes. The light was still stupidly bright but she squinted against it. His brown eyes were filled with worry and she hated that. But she knew that she was terrifying him right now. Hell, she was scaring herself a little bit. Underneath the pain and sadness she was scared, and she didn't want to think about that.

"There's my girl." He gave a small smile and reached over to give her hand a squeeze. "I was wondering if you would open your eyes again."

"It's bright as fuck in here," she said as justification.

Without hesitation he reached up and switched off the light. He took her hand again but this time did not let it go. "There, now you can keep your eyes open."

"And see nothing," she mumbled but she was grateful for the darkness. She struggled to push herself back enough so she was leaning against the door again and settled into the position.

"Take it or leave it." He heard her hiss out a breath as she settled but just gave her hand a squeeze. "Now, do you want to talk about it?"

She couldn't help but smile a little at that. He never asked directly. He always gave her the choice. He wouldn't press, but he would ask until she was ready to tell him. He was persistent but he was patient.

"I don't even know what 'it' is. I have no clue why she went off like that."

He drew in a breath and reminded himself that he would keep his temper in check. "I have no clue. I know she's never been your biggest fan. The others have said as much. But I wouldn't have ever pictured her saying those things. I don't even want to think about what she said."

"I can't stop thinking about it," she muttered, feeling the tears build back up. "It's not the first time I've heard them."

"Darlin'..." He moved so they were side by side, so he could pull her against him and wrap an arm around her waist. "I ain't supposed to hit girls, but I'll make an exception if you want me to."

She buried her face against his shirt, drew in the familiar scent of him. Soap and motor oil – he always smelled like that no matter what he'd been up to. She smiled, even as the silent tears continued to fall. "Your mum would kill you if you touched a hair on her head."

"Better plan." He pressed a kiss to her hair, an unconscious gesture. "Tell mum about it and let her deal with Anna."

"Brilliant."

"And what are we going to do about you?"

"When I figure it out I'll let you know?" She glanced up at him, her eyes red-rimmed and tear swollen. He could barely make it out in the dim light that seeped through from under the door.

"Well, for now, let's get you home and into bed." He drew her carefully to her feet, hoping that the meds would have started to numb some of the pain. "You think you'll manage the 10 minute ride?"

She nodded, her legs unsteady beneath her. She kept her arm looped through Coop's as they wound their way back through the house. It was still empty, but that wasn't surprising considering the fireworks they could hear exploding outside. Coop helped her into his jacket since hers was out on the lawn. And they headed out to his bike.

Without looking back, they left his family to enjoy the celebration, driving off while fireworks filled the sky.

Chapter 27

Five Years Ago…

She took the lasagna out of the oven, taking a moment to savour the smell of it. Setting it on the counter to cool she put the tray of garlic bread in its place and closed the oven up. By the time the garlic bread was toasted, the lasagna would be ready to eat.

It wasn't often that she went to much effort cooking dinner, but her mama would be home early from work today and her dad said he'd be back in time. So, she'd finished her homework and set to work making a meal. Not that they would expect it, but she figured it would be a nice gesture. It had been a long time since they had all sat down for a family dinner.

The early January weather brought cold, but it was hard to convince snow to come to Senoia. Still, it was dark outside despite being only six in the afternoon and she wished she had more than the radio for company.

Her mind went to Cooper who was no doubt sitting down for dinner with his family as he did almost every night, provided her dad had let him go from the shop. She hoped he had. Evie hated when Coop missed dinner. And she hoped her father was on his way home anyway. He wouldn't much like the cold garlic bread.

She would see Coop tomorrow at school. He would pick her up and they would ride in together on the back of his Rebel, much to her mama's displeasure. But it was quicker than taking the bus. And it was better than the bus. Hell, anything was better than being on that bus.

She'd been skeptical about the bike at first. When she compared it to her reliable car, she didn't see the benefits. But after her first ride, she had understood completely. There was a freedom that the bike allowed for that she could never achieve behind the wheel of her car, no matter how fast she drove it. And she wasn't shy about putting her foot down.

The sound of the door opening shocked her out of her train of thought and she glanced over to see her father stumble through it. She noticed his red face before the smell of liquor hit her. She'd had half a second to think that perhaps it was colder than she'd originally thought out then she accepted that he was drunk. Again.

"Dinner's almost ready, dad," she said turning back to the stove to peer in at the garlic bread. The cheese was melting nicely. "Mama should be home soon."

"Huh," he grunted as acknowledgement as he fought to get his scarf off. The damn thing felt like it was choking him. "You cook that?"

Darcy glanced at the lasagna that was almost cooled enough to cut. "Yes, sir."

"Looks like shit." He curled his nose in disgust. "Perhaps if you spent more time in the kitchen and less pretending to be a boy you'd learn to cook."

She closed her eyes and let the insult roll over her. As far as they went, it was mild. "I promise it tastes better than it looks." She offered him a smile. "Why don't ya have a seat, dad. You've had a long day."

"Don't patronize me, you worthless little cunt." He tossed his coat in the direction of the hooks and it tumbled to the floor. "If you want to be useful, get me drink and shut the fuck up."

"How about I get you a plate of this?" she countered, ignoring him. "Food will do you some good and mama won't mind if we start without her."

She saw him cross the room in two long strides and knew she had pushed it too far.

"I don't want a plate of your slop. I said get me a drink. Or can you not even manage that?"

"I think you've had enough to drink, dad," she said, her voice firm.

The backhand caught her clean across the mouth and she felt the pain explode through her face. Blood filled her mouth as her lip split, but she managed to keep to her feet. She had to grab the counter for balance, but she didn't fall over.

"You useless little bitch. You waste of space! You should have never been born. You were a fucking mistake."

His face was redder now. Beads of sweat were forming on his brow as he screamed at her. His breath reeked of liquor and she wanted nothing more than to get away from it but there was nowhere to go. He had her caged in against the stove and the counter.

Her hands shook at her sides and she bit her lip, causing more blood to pour from the cut. She had nothing to say to him. She was frozen. All she could do was stand there and pray that he wouldn't hit her again.

"You selfish little whore. Always trying to make me look bad." He narrowed his eyes at her. "I never wanted you. And now I can never get rid of you."

She tried to bite back the whimper that was building up in her throat. She didn't want to cry in front of him. She'd promised herself years ago that she'd never do that again. But the whimper escaped despite her best efforts. And she cursed herself for it.

"Are you going to cry?" He laughed. "Cry like the whiny little bitch you are. You're the reason everything goes wrong. You're the reason we have to work so much while you're off with those rich friends of yours all the time. You greedy, needy little bitch. I should have –"

"Andy!"

He jolted out of his stance, interrupted mid-rant by Olivia coming home from work. Neither of them had heard her come into the house.

"Don't you start with me too, Liv." He sent her a rage-filled glare then stomped over to his chair in the living room.

Liv hurried over to her daughter, dropping her purse on the way. She reached out to Darcy but she stepped away from her mother's touch. Liv let her hands drop to her sides and let out a shaky breath. "Are you alright?"

"There's lasagna on the counter." Darcy blinked back the tears that threatened to fall and clenched her shaking hands. "There was garlic bread, but it's burnt now." She stepped around her mother and towards the door. She barely thought to grab her coat before reaching for the handle.

"I won't be home tonight."

She left the apartment without looking back.

* * *

Present Day...

She was in a drug-induced sleep. He'd tucked her into his bed, closed the door, and left her there. He'd wanted to stay with her but right now she needed to sleep. He would check on her in a few hours when she needed to take more meds. If she was awake, he'd see that she took them. If she was still sleeping, he'd leave her be.

Right now, it was more important that he was awake and in the kitchen as opposed to hiding out in his bedroom with Darcy. His family would be home soon. The fireworks had ended just after he'd tucked her in and he knew they'd be headed back.

Anna had to get Mia to bed. And besides that, word of what had passed between Anna and Darcy would have spread quickly throughout the crowd. Things like that didn't stay quiet. He'd been shocked the big house had been empty when they'd left it. But he was glad for it. It would have been impossible to get Darcy through a group of people.

He set a pot of coffee to brew and settled down at the kitchen table. He wasn't a fan of waiting, but he'd learned patience early on in life. It required patience to grow up in a house filled with women. It required patience to be a mechanic. And it required a great deal of patience to deal with Darcy's pigheadedness on a regular basis.

He smiled at that last thought. She was stubborn as a mule, but he loved her for it. She'd been like that as long as he'd known her and that was one of the reasons they'd become friends. She was the toughest girl he'd ever met, and that hadn't changed. It broke his heart to see her like this.

The front door opened just as the coffee finished brewing. His family had impeccable timing, as always. He was just taking down mugs when Bea raced around the corner.

"Where is she? Is she okay? What the fuck did Anna do to her?!"

Coop set down the mug he was holding so he wouldn't throw it as the anger he hadn't quite put aside rose back up. "Darcy is fine. She's taken her meds and is downstairs resting. As for Anna," he paused as Beth joined them in the kitchen, "I'd rather not repeat what she said."

"Mum is livid." Beth turned the kettle on and dropped a teabag into one of the mugs. "I mean, I've seen her mad before but I've never seen her like this. We should probably take these elsewhere if we want to avoid the blowup."

"Where's everyone else?" Coop poured coffee into a mug so he could do something with his hands.

"Alice and Charlie stayed behind with Da to help with cleanup. Mum is on her way back with Anna, Drew, and Mia." Bea poured her own coffee and added three spoonfuls of sugar. "I agree with Beth, we should take cover."

Coop had been weighing the pros and cons of confronting his sister. He didn't know if he wanted to have it out with her. He didn't know if he could speak rationally with her at the moment. He didn't know if he could look at her without wanting to hit her.

He drew in a deep breath and let it out slowly. "Fine, I'm gonna go downstairs till the dust settles."

Bea and Beth exchanged a look.

"I think we'll just crash." Bea gave him a kiss on the cheek. "Good luck, bro. Don't kill anyone."

Beth followed her sister's gesture and then followed her upstairs. Coop watched them for a moment before heaving a sigh. He'd never understand them, but he'd always be glad to have them in his life. With that in mind, he headed downstairs to wait out the impending battle.

* * *

Evie waited. Anna was putting Mia to bed and Drew had gone downstairs to find Coop. So, Evie filled a mug with coffee and waited at the table. She knew that Anna would come back downstairs and face her. The girl was a lot of things, but she wasn't a coward.

She'd heard what had happened between Anna and Darcy. She didn't know exactly what had been said but she'd gotten the gist of it from Jimmy and Malcolm, both who had been shocked and confused to see their niece act that way. Sure, Anna was prickly but she was good-natured. And when it came to family, she was as protective as a mother bear with her cubs.

Alice had also found Evie later and given her a more in-depth version. She'd offered a bit of insight into the outburst and informed Evie that she would once again be a grandmother. Despite her happiness over that piece of information, she wasn't going to excuse Anna's behaviour. There was clearly something that needed to be addressed here. Something that hadn't been handled by their earlier conversation.

She heard Anna come down the stairs and took a moment to gather her thoughts. She loved her daughter. She loved all of her children. But Darcy was as much her daughter as the woman walking into the kitchen. And she would be damned it this would continue any longer.

"The coffee's fresh if you want some," she said sipping her own. "And then you're gonna sit down and we're gonna have a little chat."

"Oh, two talks in one day. Aren't I lucky," Anna muttered as she went to the counter to pour coffee into a mug.

"Don't you sass me, girl. I've had just about enough of your smart mouth for one day." Evie set her coffee down with a bang. "You're gonna sit down and you're gonna listen. Because whatever is going on here ends tonight, ya hear?"

Anna didn't respond. She topped off her coffee with milk because she had the luxury of it at the moment and joined her mother at the table.

Evie waited for her to say something. When she remained silent and staring into her coffee mug, she pressed on. "Now, we talked this morning about your issues with Darcy."

"I –" she began but one look at her mother stopped her dead.

"I told you that I would have no more of this nonsense from you. I thought we were clear on it. Then I hear you went at that poor girl while everyone was havin' a good time and enjoying Canada Day." Evie shook her head, still trying to wrap her mind around it. "What the devil has gotten into you? And don't go blaming this on being pregnant because this goes much further back than that." She took another sip of her coffee. "We'll talk about that later, by the way."

"I...um..." Anna ran a hand over her hair, pulling it out of its tail along the way. She could feel the migraine building and wanted nothing more than to go to bed. She wanted to forget today had ever happened. She wanted the words to go back into her head and not come out. But she knew it was too late to take them back.

"You're an articulate, intelligent, beautiful woman, Anna. You're a police officer. And we're proud of you. We love you." Evie reached across the table and took her daughter's hand. "So, why do you feel you need to destroy that poor girl? Where does all that resentment come from?"

Anna gave her mother's hand a squeeze and continued to stare into her coffee. "You've always treated her different. You and Coop. Not that you've meant to, I don't think and I don't blame you. But she always took the spotlight when she came over. You always made sure she had everything she needed, always checked up on her, always checked in with her."

"So, this is jealousy?" Evie wasn't angry right now. She was just trying to understand.

"When I was younger maybe." Anna gave a half shrug not quite happy with the descriptor. "Then I just didn't like it. The way she always took. Time, money, things – she never had anything to offer. The way Coop ran off with her. The way you still seemed so concerned about her. She was taking advantage. And I've never liked it one bit."

Evie sighed. She'd always known that keeping certain things from her children would come back to bite her. But there were things that you didn't discuss with children. Even if they were happening to a child in your own home. Children were meant to be protected, at least to a certain extent. And the Devil take her if she was going to darken her doorstep with stories about what happened at the van Dyke house.

"Now you look here, Annabelle." She watched the younger woman's gaze lift and meet hers. "That girl has never taken advantage of anything a day in her life."

"Mum –"

Evie held her free hand for silence. "I told you to listen. I'm gonna tell you a story that I've got no right tellin' and you've got no right to repeat. But ya need to hear it. If we're gonna put all this nonsense to rest you need to know the truth when it comes to Darcy."

Anna's eyes narrowed as her instincts kicked in. "You hinted at this earlier. What haven't you been telling us?"

"Well, I'd have to go back to the beginning…"

Chapter 28

Charlie and Alice left their dad in the driveway with a car full of dirty dishes. Charlie had got the message from Coop to meet him in the basement, so they bypassed the front door and rounded to the back patio entrance. The basement rec-room was lit up, the TV was playing reruns of The Simpsons, and Coop and Drew were sprawled out on the couches. They both jumped up when the girls entered.

"Took ya long enough," Coop snapped getting up from the couch.

Charlie crossed the room and took the place he abandoned. "You try cleaning up after a hundred people. It's no walk in the park."

"Where is she?" Alice glanced towards Coop's closed bedroom door and watched him nod.

"She's sleeping right now. I checked on her five minutes ago." He ran a hand through his hair and glanced over at Drew. He'd been shocked to see the man come down the stairs. Surprised to hear him ask how Darcy was doing. He'd figured that he'd take his wife's side in all this.

When Coop had asked him about it Drew had replied, "There are no sides in all this, just what's right. And making sure she's okay is the right thing to do."

Coop could respect the man for that. So, they'd turned on the TV and waited for the others to get home. Because neither of them was brave enough to go upstairs and interfere with that. Some battles had to be fought alone.

"She took the meds, right?" Charlie asked from the couch. She was nibbling at her thumbnail, a nervous habit she'd had since she was little. She didn't bite her nails, chewing them down to the quick like some people, but they always found their way to her mouth when she was nervous.

"That's the only reason she's asleep right now." Coop sighed and sunk down onto the arm of the couch. "She didn't sleep last night because she didn't want to wake anyone up. And she didn't take anything other than the extra strength Tylenol today because she didn't want to pass out."

"Didn't want to wake anyone up?" Drew leaned forward, resting his chin on his hand. "What d'you mean?"

Coop looked at Alice, not wanting to say anything, not wanting to betray Darcy that way.

"Night-terrors," Alice explained. "Common after trauma." She picked up Coop's now cold coffee and took a swallow. "Patients often relive that accident or experience high levels of anxiety when they sleep because they are vulnerable."

"Like PTSD?" Drew shrugged at her raised brow look. "I've got a brother who served in Iraq. I'm not new to the trauma bit." He glanced towards the closed door. "Poor thing. No one should go through that."

"She's in a lot of pain."

Everyone glanced over at Charlie who had said it in such a matter of fact tone. She shrugged at the attention. "I don't just know soccer, okay? I finished my kinesiology and chiropractic degree. I know pain." She glanced down at her hands remembering Darcy that morning. "She's in a world of pain and she's trying her best to hide it."

"I'll agree to that." Drew nodded, leaning back into the couch cushions. "She ran off after breakfast and I went to go check on her."

Coop looked over at him surprised. "You did?"

"I told you, I've got no problem with her. Whatever issue Anna has is hers to sort out." He held up his hands in surrender. "I told her I just needed the bathroom, but I was there to check on her. And man did she look terrible. You should have seen her before she had a chance to toss on some makeup and take a breather."

Coop thought back to Darcy on the floor of his grandparent's bathroom. If she had looked even half as bad as she had then it would have been a sight. His hands closed into fists as the image flooded back into his mind. He didn't want to think of her like that. He didn't want to remember how helpless he'd felt.

"She's not taking her meds properly. She half-ass applies her cream. And she sort of does her range of motion exercises." Alice blew out a frustrated breath. "She's not a cooperative patient, but I've dealt with worse. And I should be monitoring her more closely. But she'll need to learn to take care of herself. We're only here for another week and then she's on her own."

"I think this is beyond what you can do, Alice." Coop waited until she would meet his gaze before continuing. "When I found her in the bathroom she was ready to give up. She just wanted me to leave her the pills and let her die." He drew in a shaky breath at the memory. "Have you ever known her to give up on anything?"

"The girl's like a dog with a bone," Charlie commented, the worry clear in her voice.

"Is psychological counselling a recommended part of her treatment?" Drew inquired from the other couch.

Alice nodded. "We were going to wait until we got back to Senoia, so she could see someone regularly. We came up here so she could focus on getting over the pain in some semblance of peace." She glanced around herself helplessly. "That didn't exactly work."

"I suggest getting her that help ASAP." Drew's voice was deadpan. "Take it from someone who knows that waiting until it's convenient can mean waiting until it's too late."

They all took in the sadness in his eyes, but they didn't comment.

"I'll put out some feelers in the morning. Most clinics will be closed but I have some personal contacts I can call." Alice downed the rest of the cold coffee. "I'll have her in an appointment by Monday. You can count on that."

Coop nodded. He knew that was really all he could ask for. It was really the best he could hope for.

"Thank you." He got up from the couch and glanced around the room meeting each face. "All of you. I'm going to go check on her again."

They watched him leave, the bedroom door closing softly behind him. Drew leaned forward and clasped his hands between his knees. He looked from the oldest sister to the youngest and a smile pulled at his lips.

"He's got it bad."

"What?" Alice, who had been mentally making a list of doctors in the area she knew, glanced over confused. "What are you talking about?"

"Give it time. He might not know it yet." Drew got to his feet, smile still in place. "But he'll figure it out soon enough."

"You're not talking about..." Charlie glanced over at the bedroom door then back at Drew. "No..." There was uncertainty in her voice.

"Give it time." He took the empty coffee mug from Alice. "Now, if you'll excuse me, I'm going to go see if my wife survived her tear down."

Alice watched him go up the stairs realizing she'd learned more about the man in the last hour than she had in three years worth of family gatherings. Life was strange that way.

Charlie left soon after without a word but Alice stayed, a pen and paper in front of her, and tried to get her head sorted before she went to sleep. Because in the morning she would have to get to work. In the morning, she would ruin a few people's Saturdays. But at the moment she couldn't care less.

* * *

Coop crawled into bed next to her after insuring she took her next dose of medication. She had woken soon after he'd come into the room. She'd been tossing and turning, tangled in the sheets, and on the verge of screaming. He'd woken her gently from the nightmare. He'd gotten her water and given her another pill.

Now, she was drifting off to sleep again, curled up next to him with her head resting on his chest. He ran a hand absently over her hair, careful not to let his arm put any pressure on her burns. He wanted to comfort her, not cause her more pain.

She was asleep again. He could tell by the even rhythm of her breathing. He knew that she would sleep for a few more hours before the dreams could touch her. So, he would sleep as well. And when she woke up, he would be there. He could do nothing else for her now, so the least he could do was be there for her.

Chapter 29

Sixteen Years Ago...

She sat with her hands clasped in her lap and fought the urge to swing her legs back and forth. Her starched dress was itchy and it was too warm in the church cramped between her mama and daddy. But she was determined to be good.

Mama had told her that if she was good then she could meet a new friend today. If she was good then she could have a play date. She hadn't had one of those before. At least not outside of Sunday school or recess. This sounded different. This sounded better.

So, she was going to sit still. She was going to behave even though the church smelled like grandma and her dress was itchy. Even though she didn't understand what the old man at the front was saying. She needed to be good so she could make a new friend.

Time passed slower than molasses. She stood when mama did and knelt when mama did and sang and sat. She didn't swing her feet. She didn't itch at her dress. And she didn't squirm in her seat. It took all of her six-year-old patience to make it through the service.

She had to try not to rush out of the church when they were dismissed. Everything was moving so slowly it seemed. When they got outside her mother greeted another woman who had a troupe of kids around her. Darcy pressed close to her mother's skirt and tried to stay out of sight.

"So good to see you, Liv." Evie kissed her friend's cheek and sent Andy a smile. "This must be your little one."

"Yes, this is Darcy." Liv patted her daughter's head. "Darcy, this is Mrs. McKnight."

"Pleased to meet you, ma'am," Darcy mumbled.

Evie grinned. The girl was adorable with her red hair and bright blue eyes. Even if she seemed a might bit shy. "And this is my son, Cooper." She grabbed his collar and pulled him forward. "Cooper, this is Mr. and Mrs. van Dyke and their daughter Darcy."

"Nice to meet you," he said to the ground. He didn't like the looks of the girl with her frilly dress and her long red hair. She looked just like his sisters and he hated playing with his sisters.

Darcy looked at the boy with his sandy hair and brown eyes. This was supposed to be her friend? He couldn't even look at adults when he talked to them.

"Now, you kids play while we chat over here by the big tree." Evie gave Coop a push forward then looped her arm through Liv's to walk off. If she knew anything about kids it was that they would get themselves sorted better if they were left alone than if they were hovered over.

Darcy eyed him for a moment standing there with his hands in his pockets looking like he'd lost something. "Your tie is crooked," she said, hands clasped behind her back.

"Well, your dress is dumb," he countered, sticking out his tongue. He received a smack with his mum's purse for that. Apparently, she hadn't been far enough away yet.

"Cooper Joseph Douglas McKnight, you behave or you'll be playin' dolls with Charlie for the next ten years," Evie threatened.

"Yuck," the kids said in unison.

He looked at her skeptically. "You don't like dolls?"

"No, they're stupid." She curled her lip in disgust and shot a look to her mother who was walking away now. Still, she whispered, "I only act happy about them to make mama happy."

He gave her a once over from her shockingly red hair to her black buckled shoes. "What kind of girl doesn't like dolls?"

Darcy reached into the pocket of her dress and pulled out the Hot Wheels she had stashed there after her mother had checked her pockets. "The kind who likes these better." She stuck her hand forward.

Coop looked at the shiny red car, eyes lighting up. "Mum tried to take mine away before we left." He pulled his own car out even as he looked closer at hers. "I don't think I have that one."

"Well, you can play with mine if I can play with yours," she offered.

He considered for a moment. He didn't have any friends who were girls other than his sisters. But she seemed okay. "Well, I suppose you'll do till I can find a better friend."

It was her turn to look skeptical. "Ain't no one in this town better."

He laughed as she placed her hands firmly on her hips trying to look put off in her white, frilly dress. "You may just be right."

* * *

Present Day...

Darcy slept straight through Saturday. She hadn't meant to and if it weren't for the meds she probably would have gotten up. But as it were, she spent the whole day in bed. Coop came and went checking in on her. Alice too. He gave her the meds when she woke up and then she would slip back off into sweet nothingness.

There was something very tempting about the nothingness. It was warm and dark and empty. There was no pain in the darkness. That was the best part. Everything was numb and muffled. When she was there she wanted nothing more than to stay. But she knew that she couldn't. She knew that there was something on the other side of it all pulling her back.

Sometimes she made it to the other side without issue. She would go from the darkness straight into Cooper's bedroom as if nothing had happened. Other times she was less lucky. Other times she detoured into her nightmares. She was trapped. She was burning. She couldn't breathe.

Those times she would wake up gasping for air. She would wake up screaming. She would wake up in a tangle of sheets soaked in sweat and disoriented. Sometimes Coop would be there and he would offer her water and another pill. Something to bring the darkness back. Sometimes she was alone and she sat shaking and crying until someone came.

Saturday was a blur of this. Medication and sleep. Darkness and nightmares. Her body, having taken a beating the previous day, was done. It would not listen to her. She could barely move when she wasn't thrashing from nightmares. Everything felt heavy and her mind felt clouded.

It had been late Saturday night when she'd managed to stay awake for more than a half hour. She'd talked Cooper into watching a movie with her and holding off on the meds for a while. The pain was still there but she could manage.

They were halfway through *Fast and Furious,* and making fun of it the whole way, when she turned to him. "I'm going to church with ya'll tomorrow."

To his benefit he didn't laugh or choke on the popcorn he was eating. He took a moment to think about how to handle his response. "Darlin' –"

"Don't darlin' me, Cooper McKnight. I'm goin' to church and that's the end of it. I've spent all day in this damn bed and I won't spend another." She crossed her arms and the effort cost her as pain radiated through her shoulders. She didn't remember the last time she'd put her cream on.

"Alright." He shook his head. She was looking better. She wasn't nearly as pale now, the shadows under her eyes were disappearing, and the meds were keeping the pain at bay. But that didn't mean he was happy about the idea of her going out.

"I'd appreciate if you got me up early enough to get ready." She frowned at the popcorn bowl between them. "I don't have any control over things with these damn meds."

He reached over and gave her hand a squeeze. "It won't always be like this."

"God, I hope not," she said with a laugh, trying to lighten the mood. He'd been treating her like she was made of glass all day and it was starting to piss her off. "Now, shut up or you're gonna talk over the big reveal."

Coop smiled but fell silent and went back to watching the movie, keeping a careful watch on her out of the corner of his eye. She would go back to sleep soon, he knew. And maybe she would sleep through the night. He hoped so because he'd have to get her up early if she planned on making it to church.

That was how she'd gotten where she was now. Standing in front of the small rustic church that put the ornate Catholic churches she was used to to shame. The father's house was in the lot next door looking just as humble. It had been years since she'd been to this church, but she could see the inside clearly in her mind's eye even as she stood outside it with Coop beside her.

It had been a painful experience getting ready for today, but she had muscled her way through it. The shower alone had almost done her in. The meds had numbed much of the pain she had felt on Friday, but the water brought it back to the surface. She'd had to brace herself against the walls of the shower to keep from falling over. Still, she had made it through.

Alice had put her cream on and given her a half dosage of her medication. She hoped it wouldn't knock her out. She'd already had two coffees just to try and counteract the drowsiness that usually came along with the pills.

The sundress she was wearing was strapless which she could be grateful for. She'd borrowed it from Bea and the light wrap from Beth who was the more modest of the two. She wasn't about to show up to church in a strapless dress. Her mama would have killed her and although Evie was a little more liberal with dress code, there were strict rules when it came to church.

She'd taken her time with her makeup and done her best to cover the pain and sleeplessness that still showed on her face. She may have spent a day in bed but she still didn't look herself yet. She was too thin, too pale, and looked too fragile. Everything about her looked like it would shatter if touched. She hated it.

She'd met Coop downstairs and found him dressed in his Sunday best. There were no corners to be cut when it came to church. The dress pants, white shirt, and tie looked out of place on him, but he still looked handsome. Duncan and Drew were with him wearing similar getups, though their shirt and tie choices provided more colour. They were quite a bunch she had a chance to think before Coop ushered her out of the house.

Now, she stood in front of the church wondering when was the last time she'd been inside one. Her father's funeral perhaps? She wasn't certain if she'd gone after that but she doubted it. She hadn't placed much faith in religion after that day.

Coop laid a hand on her arm, which were currently crossed. She glanced up at him, her eyes still a little distant. "You don't have to go in there."

"Like hell," she muttered but there was a smile on her face. "Your mum might give me a pass this time, but I'm not gonna piss anyone else off this holiday."

Coop had to force himself not to ball his hand into a fist. He'd had it out with Anna and his mum while she was asleep yesterday. It was sorted. But that didn't mean he had to be happy about it. "I don't give a fuck about the rest of them right now."

Her brow rose at his tone. "They're your family, Coop."

"And so are you." He ran his hands through his hair in frustration. "I've known you since you were six years old, Darcy." He let out a helpless sigh. "You matter."

She bit her lip and stared at the ground. It wasn't exactly an old argument, but recently his family had been an area of contention between them. Ever since they'd hit the road together three years ago they'd circled the topic. It was only recently that they'd gotten around to addressing it.

"Can we just go into the church, Coop?" She glanced up at him. She could see the frustration in his eyes and wondered if they could avoid further argument. "I just want to sit in our pew and listen to the service like everyone else. I just want to be normal for a few hours."

He nodded and linked her arm with his. "You know we can't sit at the back, right?"

She laughed as they walked into the church arm in arm. "If only it was so easy." She followed him to the second pew from the front on the right side. It belonged to the McKnights and had for decades. It was the only time she'd ever been to a church where pews were reserved.

"It's not too late to run away," he whispered as more people filed through the door. He glanced back to see his parents with Drew, Anna, and Mia.

Darcy followed his gaze and fought the wave of anxiety that flooded through her. She met his eyes, those familiar brown eyes that had gotten her through so many things in life. She gave a small smile as the woman at the piano began to warm up. "Never."

Chapter 30

She made it through church. There wasn't much time or space for name-calling or harassment when the whole family separated them and the priest never stopped talking. She had missed the ritual of it. Church had always been something she had shared with her mama. For as long as she could remember.

Then mama had gotten sick and she couldn't make it to church anymore. Darcy had stopped going as well. She'd started working more. She'd started racing. Anything to bring money in. Anything to help out. And anything to get her out of the house.

She regretted that now. She regretted that she had wanted to run away from her mama when she'd been sick. That her being sick had scared her. But she'd barely been eighteen. She'd still been in school. She didn't know better.

Her father had known better but that didn't stop him from spending all his time away. Working, he would say. But she knew he was doing more drinking than working. She knew that Coop had done most of the work in that last year. That all the money her father had brought in had gone to liquor.

She shook her head and tried to dismiss the thoughts. She didn't want to worry about old memories right now. She had enough things to deal with. But it was hard not to remember when sitting in that church pew had been so familiar.

Now, she was back at the house. She'd slept for a few hours, courtesy of the medication Alice had insisted she take, and when she'd woken Anna, Drew, and Mia had left. She was sad that she hadn't been able to say goodbye to Mia, but with the tension currently it was best she'd slept through their departure.

She wasn't sure what to think about Anna. She still couldn't wrap her mind around the words that had been said over the campfire. She had so many other things to worry about not to add Anna's opinion of her to the pile. But damnit, her opinion mattered. She was Coop's sister. So, even if she'd always been prickly, her opinion was important.

Darcy didn't want to be an imposition on anyone. She had always felt a little out of place with the McKnights, a little like she didn't quite belong. It was nothing they had ever done. It was completely her. But this was the first time any one of them had expressed a displeasure with her presence. She didn't know how to handle it. She didn't know what to think about it. It was like having her own beliefs realized. Her own insecurities thrown in her face.

She ran a hand through her hair, making it more of a mess than it already was. She was alone in the living room. She wasn't certain where everyone else was but there was noise from the kitchen. If she was to hazard a guess they would be preparing Sunday dinner. One more ritual before everyone disbanded after the holiday.

She smiled at the thought. It had been a long time since she'd had Sunday dinner.

She found Beth and Bea at the counter preparing potatoes for the barbecue. Alice and Evie were working on a salad. And Coop was cutting a roast into steaks. Duncan was hiding somewhere, likely buried in work. He would emerge for dinner but until then would stay scarce.

"Where's Charlie?" Darcy leaned against the door jam casually taking in the scene.

Bea sent her a sympathetic glance. “She had to head out. Something about an early practice Monday and with the flight it’s going to be a stupid trip back.”

Darcy sighed. “I missed half the family leaving.”

“Well, you get to see me off,” Beth said cheerfully. “I’m leaving after dinner.”

“I guess there’s that.” Darcy attempted a smile. “Anything I can do to help?”

Evie glanced around herself, looking at the assembly line that usually formed in the kitchen. The benefit of having so many children. “You can set the table, deary.”

Darcy nodded and went to the cupboard to retrieve plates. She sent Coop a smile as he headed out to the deck with the plate of steaks and a bottle of barbecue sauce. She would rather have his job but she’d learned early on to take whatever job Evie handed to you.

She felt good. She was a little groggy and the plates felt as though they weighed ten tones in her sluggish arms, but overall she felt good. The meds had lowered her pain level to a dull ache, which was nothing compared to what it had been the other day. And her movement was better thanks to the cream. She wasn’t perfect, and she was a long way from what she used to be, but she was feeling better.

She heard the smash before she realized the plates had fallen out of her hands. She’d barely taken two steps away from the cupboard. She didn’t step back from the broken glass. She couldn’t. All she could do was stare down at her hands with confusion. She flexed them experimentally and wondered what the fuck had happened.

Evie reacted immediately, turning around from her place at the counter and looking over at Darcy. The girl was sheet white, staring at her hands as if they were foreign objects. She was standing in a sea of shattered plates.

"You alright, Darcy?" She kept her voice level. She didn't give a damn about the plates. "Beatrice, go fetch the broom."

"I'm sorry about your plates." Darcy continued to stare at her hands, continued to flex them slowly. "I don't know what happened."

Coop rushed through the doorway off the deck. "I heard a crash..." he trailed off as his eyes fell on Darcy. He hurried to her, reaching out to lay a hand on her arm. "Are you okay?"

"I'm not a Goddamn child." She stepped away from him. Her eyes burned with the tears she wouldn't let fall. "I just dropped some plates is all. I'm just clumsy." She rubbed her hands over her face trying to compose herself.

Bea came back with the broom. "No trouble, we'll get it all cleaned up." She offered Darcy a smile. "Just make sure you don't have any glass in your feet before you keep walking around."

She glanced down at the ground where she was standing. She hadn't even realized that she was on top of glass shards. She bit back the curse that sprang to her lips and glanced over at Alice who was watching her closely.

"Care to make a comment, doctor?"

Alice pursed her lips and wondered why Darcy had to be so difficult. She was standing there, almost in tears and she still would snap at anyone who dared talk to her as if she was injured.

Coop grabbed her by the elbows and lifted her clear of the debris before she had a chance to protest. He was shocked by how light she was now. She'd never been heavy, but she'd been solid. The woman he set down in the kitchen chair felt as fragile as the broken china on the floor.

His brow furrowed in worry and confusion, but Alice was already moving around the debris to check on her feet. She crouched down in front of her and lifted a foot onto her knee. "Let's see what damage you managed to do."

"I can take care of my –" The look Alice shot her had the words she'd been about to say dying in her mouth.

"Coop, you might want to check those steaks before they burn," Evie commented from her place back at the counter were she was piling potatoes on a plate.

"I didn't put them on yet," Coop said absently, hovering behind Darcy's chair.

"Then take these out and put them on." Evie passed him the plate, careful to avoid the remaining pieces of glass.

"You're hovering, Coop." Bea sent him a smile as she carried a dustpan full of glass to the garbage.

He sent her a glare but took the plate and did as he was told. There was no use arguing with his mother. It never worked.

Alice inspected both of Darcy's feet and found them free of cuts. She'd been lucky. "Have your hands gone numb like that before?" She took Darcy's hands and examined them. "Flex please."

Darcy did as instructed. "No, I've never had anything like that happen before." She bit her lip and tried not to worry about it too much. "Most everything feels sluggish after I take the meds. Is this because of them?"

Alice continued to test Darcy's reflexes moving up her body then back down. "It could be," she muttered sitting back on her heels. "It's hard to say how pain killers like that will affect a person."

"Well, no harm done." Evie sent her a smile, her eyes sympathetic. "They're just plates after all. Got plenty more."

Darcy nodded but that didn't stop the guilt that welled up inside her. "I think someone else should set the table. I'm a bit of a hazard right now." She pushed to her feet and was surprised that her legs held her up. "I think I'll go outside with Coop."

Evie watched her leave and let out a sigh. "Whatever am I gonna do with that girl."

"You got her into an appointment on Monday, right Alice?" Beth, who had been silent thus far, inquired. She was leaning against the counter taking in the scene in her usual assessing way.

Alice nodded, getting to her feet. "Yeah. I managed to find someone with an opening." She ran a hand through her hair. "It's not a perfect solution, but it will give us a start for when she goes back to Senoia. And we need to start somewhere."

"She's been through more than anyone should at her age," Evie muttered going back to chopping vegetables for the salad.

"That's usually the case." Alice shrugged. She needed to stop thinking of Darcy as family and start to look at her as her patient. She was overlooking things. She was slipping up as she got caught up in the family dynamic of it all. And that needed to stop. "But she'll get through it. She's resilient."

"Oh, I have no doubt about that." Evie glanced towards the doors Darcy had left through. "She's stubborn as a mule as well."

"Wonder where she learned that?" Bea muttered.

"You sassing me?" Evie waved her knife accusingly.

"Wouldn't dream of it." Bea grinned and sent her twin an eye roll. "Can we just make it through Sunday dinner without fighting? I've had enough bickering for one family holiday."

Evie let out a heavy sigh. "You know Anna didn't really mean it."

"I don't want to talk about it," Bea said firmly. "Or think about it. Ever."

"I concur," Alice said, grimacing.

"Fine, we'll shelve it for the time being."

"Forever," Beth corrected. "That's the consensus."

"And since when do we live in a democracy?" Evie raised a brow.

"Since you raised intelligent and free-thinking daughters." Bea gave her mother a kiss on the cheek as she walked by to put the broom back. "I'll finish setting the table."

Chapter 31

He would let her sleep. She was going to need it for today and it had been a trial getting her to sleep to begin with. Despite the medication, the nightmares had been persistent. She'd woken up screaming once and the second time she'd been gasping for breath.

He'd be lying if he said it wasn't wearing on him. But he knew that it was taking a bigger toll on her. He didn't know what she saw when she closed her eyes, but he had a pretty good idea. Similar images made his heart race in the middle of the night and sent him into a panic. But still, she had it worse.

Alice had made her an appointment with a doctor in Halifax today. With some persuasion and bribery the doctor had fit Darcy into his schedule for the afternoon. But it was a matter of getting her there that he was concerned about.

She wasn't going to go willingly. He remembered her in the hospital. He remembered her skepticism. He remembered the look of a caged animal on her face. There was fear there. And it wasn't completely unwarranted. She didn't have a good history with the medical system. It had done very little to help her in the past.

He glanced over at her as she slept, curled into a protective ball on her good side. He'd seen her sleep like that a thousand times. As if she was always trying to protect herself from something or someone. An unconscious habit, he supposed, after years of the world being cruel to her. Of needing to protect herself from it.

He wanted to run a hand over her hair. He wanted to pull her close and assure her that she was fine and safe. But he did neither of those things. Gestures like that were fine when she awoke in the dark from a nightmare, but they had no place in the early morning light.

Instead, he left the bed and headed towards the kitchen where he knew that coffee would be waiting. That was one thing he could always count on when his parents were around. Coffee was made before any reasonable person should be awake and he often wondered if his father even slept.

As expected, he found Duncan at the kitchen table, a half eaten muffin in front of him and an empty coffee mug beside it. There was stubble on his cheeks and his hair was ruffled from running his hands through it. His reading glasses, which he'd only needed recently, were perched on the end of his nose and his tall frame was hunched over his laptop.

"Need a refill?" Coop scooped up his coffee mug and chuckled when he jolted. "Or maybe you should lay off the caffeine, da."

Duncan smiled, a little sheepishly, as he stretched in his chair. He had no clue how long he'd been sitting there. His glance at the clock had him wincing. "Maybe tea would be a better choice."

"Did you sleep at all?" Coop set the kettle to boil and leaned against the counter with his own full mug of coffee.

Duncan eyed the mug jealously but knew that he'd start vibrating if he put any more coffee into his system. "I caught a nap on the couch. Your mum will be pissed I didn't come to bed last night, but I got caught up."

"You always do."

He shrugged. "New project. I want to get it wrapped up quickly and off my plate. I don't particularly like doing it."

Coop picked up a muffin from the container on the counter and took a generous bite. "Then why did you take the job?" he asked over his mouthful.

"I like to work." He shrugged again. "And I owed someone a favour."

"That'll do it." Coop chuckled as he joined his father at the table. "Will you be square after this is done?"

"One can hope." The kettle began to whistle and Duncan got up from the table to fix his tea. "I hear you're on a great adventure today."

"Top secret mission more like it."

"She doesn't know?" Warm mug in hand he rejoined his son at the table. "Well, I suppose that makes sense. She wouldn't go if she knew."

"You always were perceptive." It was Coop's turn to shrug. "She needs to go. She needs to talk to someone. Someone other than me. "

Duncan nodded. "It's a lot for one person to handle." He waited for his son to meet his gaze. "Especially when that person is battling their own demons."

"Da –"

"Don't give me some crap about how you're not. You don't go through that and come out clean." He shook his head. "That's not how it works."

"She went through a lot worse than I did, da. I can handle my own demons until she gets hers sorted." Coop stared down at his hands, examining the pink and white lines on them from where the fire had kissed his skin. "She needs me to be strong for her."

"And I need you to be honest with me." Again he waited for Coop to glance up. "Are you okay?"

He let out a shaky breath and struggled to hold his dad's scrutinizing gaze. The man saw more than people gave him credit for. Coop often forgot that.

"No. I'm far from okay." He ran a hand through his hair and gave a nervous laugh. "I don't know how to be okay after all of this."

Duncan placed a hand on his shoulder and gave it a reassuring squeeze. "We're here for you, if you need us. Know that. I don't care if you think she needs you to be strong. That macho crap has never flown well in this house. We're outnumbered," he said the last part in a conspiratorial whisper that had Coop laughing.

"I kind of noticed that." He downed some more of his coffee. "And it has nothing to do with macho crap. She doesn't really trust anyone else."

Duncan nodded. He knew enough about the girl to understand that. "Well regardless, we are here. For whatever you need."

"Thanks, da. I appreciate it."

Duncan gave his son's shoulder one more squeeze before getting to his feet. "Now, if you'll excuse me, I should go find your mum before she murders me."

"Best of luck." Coop toasted him with his mug before emptying it.

"I may need it." Duncan left Coop at the kitchen table, staring at his coffee mug and hoped he had gotten through. He could tell the boy was suffering. It was written all over his face. He just wanted to make sure he didn't suffer alone.

So, like any other time when he was confused about something, Duncan sought out the one person who seemed to clarify everything for him. He went to find Evie.

* * *

Darcy found them in the kitchen. It was the central meeting place of every house. She had always believed that. It had always been the truth for the McKnight family.

They were huddled around the table, coffee mugs filled and assorted breakfast items in front of them. They were arguing baseball, which was a common debate in the summer time. Once winter rolled around it would be nothing but hockey.

Darcy had grown up in a football and NASCAR household, so it had been a change of pace for her. But she had adjusted well and she had adjusted quickly. Because she'd wanted nothing more than to fit in with them, to fit in somewhere. Plus, she hated football. It was practically un-American of her, she knew, but she figured as long as she had racing and baseball no one would exile her.

She watched Duncan struggle to try to provide commentary on the latest game. He always put in an honest effort but he could never really get his sports straight. He never bothered to keep up. But he always tried.

"He's not part of the team anymore," Darcy corrected as she came into the kitchen and headed towards the coffee pot. She still felt groggy and sluggish from the meds, but the caffeine would help. "But he was great when he was."

Bea chuckled as she passed her own mug over for a refill. "It would help if he actually watched the games with the sound on. Then he might know the player's names."

Duncan shrugged. His laptop was away now that everyone was at the table. Evie wouldn't stand for him puttering away at it during family breakfast. She demanded that he partake in the social aspects of the family, even if they were chaotic.

"At least he watches them and doesn't just pretend he does," Coop shot a meaningful look at Alice who was picking at her muffin.

She sent him a glare. "Like I have time to watch baseball. I barely have time to breathe when I'm on shift. You're lucky I check the scores so I can follow the conversation."

"I'm just glad she learned the team names finally," Darcy said with a smile. "It was getting a little embarrassing."

"Not nearly as embarrassing as your fashion sense was when I first met you," Alice countered, sipping her coffee to hide her grin.

"Touché." Darcy gave her a mock salute.

"Now girls, play nice," Evie chuckled, taking her husband's hand on the table. She enjoyed this normalcy. It was nice to see after the weekend they'd had.

"Where's the fun in that," Darcy muttered and felt Coop kick her in the shin under the table.

"That was a nice segway into our adventure for today, Alice. Though it was sassier than necessary." Bea shot her a look. "We're gonna go into the city for a shopping adventure."

"Shopping?" Darcy cast a skeptical look from one face to the other before settling on Coop's. "You in on this scheme?"

"I figured a day out would be good for you." He winced as she glared at him. "Figured normal would be good."

"It was my idea." Bea came to his rescue. "I wanted a girls day with you before I left."

"You're leaving?" Darcy's hand jolted on her coffee mug. If there had been any left in it then it would have spilt on the table.

"Well, not this second." She sent a glance at Evie. "But I suppose I'll have to find something, eventually. I can't mooch off the parentals forever."

"Hasn't stopped you so far," Duncan muttered into his mug and had his wife chuckling.

"You play nice too," she chastised but there was a smile on her face. "And I think a shopping day would do everyone some good. It would give Duncan some time alone to work and it'll get us all out to the city."

"Everybody's going?"

Bea nodded. "We'll take the car and you can ride with Coop." She smiled winningly. "Look happier, Darcy. It'll be fun."

"Oh yeah," she muttered rubbing her hands over her face. "Fun."

Chapter 32

She knew they weren't going to the mall the minute they hit Halifax. The car went in one direction and the bike went in another. Sure, they could have been taking a detour. But she felt the anxiety rip through her the minute the two vehicles separated. Her grip around Coop tightened, but she knew that she had no control over where they were headed.

When they pulled into the plaza and parked in front of the small clinic, she felt the anxiety spike into full-blown terror. The bike came to a stop and she was off it before the engine could shut off.

"What the fuck is this, Coop?" She stood two parking spaces away from him, her hands held up to ward him off.

Coop still sat on the bike. He removed his helmet slowly and turned to face her. He'd known this wouldn't go well. But he'd hoped they'd make it inside before she freaked out. "Will you at least give it a try?"

She tossed her helmet at him and was mildly satisfied when he fumbled to catch it. "So, what? The others get to go shopping and you get to escort me to the loony bin?"

"Don't be dramatic, darlin'. It's not like you." He set the spare helmet down behind him and swung off the bike. "You need to talk to someone."

"Like hell I do." She took a step back even as he took one forward. "I talk to you, don't I? I talk to Bea! Why do I have to go talk to a stranger about something that is none of his, or her, damn business?"

He ran a hand through his hair and resisted the urge to toss her over his shoulder and cart her into the office. It wouldn't be the first time he'd done it in her life. But he knew that if she went through those doors it had to be her choice.

"Alice went to a lot of trouble to set up this appointment, Darcy. Called in a lot of favours. The least you can do is see it through." He met her gaze, saw the anger in it warring with the guilt. "If you won't do it for yourself then do it for her."

"Low blow, McKnight." She glared at him as she chewed on her lower lip. No part of her wanted to see what the inside of that office looked like.

"Learned from the best." He offered a small smile as he scooped up the helmets, partially so they wouldn't get taken and partially so she couldn't escape. He tossed a glance at her as he headed towards the doors. "Are you coming or are you gonna stand in that parking space for the next hour?"

She looked at the clinic and felt her stomach do one lazy somersault. "I hate you."

"No you don't." He took her hand when she reached his side. "But I'm willing to indulge that fantasy for a little while if it'll get you through the door."

Darcy didn't reply, but she gripped his hand tightly. If she had to use him as a life line right now, she would. She didn't trust herself not to run in the opposite direction and not look back. She barely trusted her legs to carry her through the door.

The office looked and smelt like every other clinic she'd been to in her life. It was a little too neat, a little too sterile, and the air fresheners did little to hide either fact. The receptionist greeted them cheerfully and gave her the basic paperwork to fill out.

Coop did it for her. Her hands were shaking so badly that she couldn't hold the pen. And after three attempts to write her name he'd taken the clipboard from her and filled out the sheet. He knew everything that needed to be written there. And if he was uncertain he asked.

He felt terrible. Seeing her like this made him want to carry her away and pretend it never happened. He hated Alice for insisting that he be the one to take her. But he also knew that she wouldn't have gone in for anyone else. He hated that he was a part of making her feel like this, but he knew it was for her own good. At least he hoped it was.

"Dr. Simms will see you now."

Darcy looked up from her hands, which were still shaking in her lap and felt her pulse triple in speed. She gave Coop a panicked look and he squeezed her hands reassuringly.

"I'll be right out here when you're done." He didn't try to smile. He kept his face sober. "We'll get ice cream after."

She thought about making a snarky comment about that, but couldn't make her mouth form the words. Instead, she simply rose to her feet and followed the receptionist down a short hall and into a medium sized office. The walls were painted in subdued tones and there was nothing that stood out about the furniture. It was meant to be calming, she supposed. But it made her feel tired.

The man inside the room surprised her. She had expected an older gentleman. But he looked to be in his thirties by his unlined face and thick black hair. His blue eyes were hidden behind thin-rimmed glasses but the colour stood out enough to be noticeable. He wasn't seated behind his desk, as she'd expected him to be. Instead, he was comfortably seated in one of two overstuffed chairs sipping his coffee.

"Have a seat, Miss van Dyke." He gestured to the chair beside him. "Can I get you a coffee?"

She nodded, not because she wanted the coffee in particular but because holding the mug would give her something to do with her hands. "Call me Darcy, please."

He gave a small smile as he poured her a mug. "Cream or sugar?"

"Sugar, thank you." She accepted the coffee as she sank into the chair. This almost felt normal. Like two people having a conversation. Like two friends catching up. If it wasn't for the ball of nerves in her stomach, she would let herself believe that.

"So, I get this call from Alice, begging me to see you," he began as he sipped his coffee. She was as nervous as a rabbit in a snare, he mused. Cut her loose and she would run until her legs gave out or her heart stopped. "So naturally, I agreed. Partially out of curiosity, and also as a favour to Alice."

"You know her?" Darcy gripped the mug so tightly she wondered if it would break.

"Let's just say we walked the same halls once upon a time." He smiled into his mug. "So, I looked into you, Darcy. Alice sent me your records and I did some digging. But what I really want to know, is if Alice should be worried."

"Aren't you supposed to figure that out?" Her brow furrowed in confusion.

"For now, I want you to talk. Tell me what's going on. And we'll go from there."

Darcy sighed heavily and shifted in the chair. "I had a bad day and everyone is blowing it out of proportion."

"Why don't you tell me about your bad day?"

She glared at him. If he wanted to know then she would tell him. "Fine. I hadn't slept because I didn't want to wake the house up with my screaming when I came out of a nightmare."

"Do you get nightmares often?"

"Only every time I close my eyes," she scoffed. "So, I was sleep deprived and in pain, because I hadn't taken my meds. Mostly because they make me sleep and then nightmares and then screaming. It's a vicious cycle."

"Do you often not take your meds?"

His calm voice was beginning to irritate her. "I take them when I want and I don't take them when I don't want to. I deal with the pain when I have to." She gave a half shrug and tried not to hiss out a breath as the pain raced across her shoulders.

"You're in pain now."

"You're observant." She rolled her eyes. "They teach you that in med school."

"How do you deal with the pain?"

"I just deal." She sent him another glare and decided maybe she wanted some of the coffee after all. "You just have to learn how to deal."

"Some people deal by causing themselves pain elsewhere. Do you do that, Darcy? Do you hurt yourself?"

She narrowed her eyes and considered him for a moment, wondering if he was serious. "Did Alice tell you I was a risk for self-harm? Is that what you're getting at? One bad day and this is what I get for it."

"Why would they think you're at risk for self-harm, Darcy?"

She chewed on her bottom lip, considered avoiding the question. "I told Coop to leave me alone with my bottle of meds so I could disappear. It was a low moment."

"Do you often have suicidal thoughts?"

She raised a brow. He looked so damn calm in that overstuffed chair. "No, I do not often have suicidal thoughts. I never have them. I'm 22. I've got a lot going on. I didn't go through fire just to snuff things out now."

"So, what was so special about that moment?"

If he'd had a pen she imagined he'd be tapping it against his lips right now. Instead, he was tapping his foot to some internal beat and it was equally annoying. "Have you ever experienced real pain, Dr. Simms? And I don't mean cut yourself or stub a toe type of pain. I mean, you would rather cut off that part of your body than have it continue to send signals to your brain type of pain. Persistent, chronic, exhausting pain. Pain that makes you throw up. Pain that makes your eyes water. Have you ever felt that?"

"I can't say I have, Darcy."

At least he had the decency to pale a bit, she thought. "Then you can't understand what its like to just want it to go away. To want to be able to sleep again without seeing the worst moments of your life. To want to be able to do your everyday things but know you can't."

"The pain will go away, Darcy. The burns will heal."

"But they will always be there. And so will the highlight reel in my head. So, you can sit in your big chair and preach if you want, Dr. Simms. But until you've lived through hell, until you've been pulled through the fire, you can't judge me."

"I'm not here to judge you." He sat back in the chair and folded his hands over his knee. "I'm here to listen and to help."

She scoffed. "How the hell are you supposed to help me?"

"Well," he considered for a moment. "I would suggest a sleeping aid for starters. To help combat the nightmares. Since your pain management is not my department, the best I can offer is to help you sleep."

"If the pain meds won't keep me down, what makes you think your sleeping pills will?" She set her mug down and crossed her arms.

"Let's just say I'm hopeful." He offered a smile. Alice was going to owe him big time for this. He never wrote prescriptions after a single consult. "I do recommend, once you're back in the States, that you seek further counselling."

"Why?"

He sighed, not remotely surprised. "Because it is part of the standard treatment for trauma victims. Because you are suffering from nightmares. Because you are perfect candidate for PTSD. The list really could go on, but that is my highlight reel."

"The sleeping pills will help?" She shifted in the chair. She still didn't like him. She didn't like being there or having to talk to him. But his offer to help her sleep was too tempting to resist. She really missed sleep.

"Yes, Darcy. They will help.

Chapter 33

It hadn't gone like she'd thought it would. By the time the hour had been up they hadn't discussed her parents or her childhood at all. They hadn't talked about her nightmares or the accident. They had just talked.

He had asked her about the pain. He had asked her about her medication. He had asked her if she liked the east coast. Whether she was rooting for the Jays this season or if she was all about the American teams. After her initial outburst, they didn't touch on her problems. They just chatted.

She was sure he was still assessing. She was sure he was still filling away everything in his head to make decisions about later. She wasn't naïve. She knew why she was there. But when she left his office she didn't feel as bad about it. In truth, she didn't know how to feel about it.

She had a prescription for sleeping pills and a promise to see someone when she got back to Senoia by the time she got on the bike with Coop. He didn't ask her how it went. He just handed her the helmet and they set off.

They made it to the mall, but they got no further than the food court. It wasn't until they were both seated with heaping ice cream cones that he slid a glance in her direction.

"So, did the useless doctor say anything useful?" He took a bite of his moose tracks ice cream, making her cringe.

"How can you do that? And why do you get ice cream that you have to chew." She licked her strawberry cone.

"Mostly to annoy you." He grinned and took another bite. "Oh and because it's delicious." He held it out to her. "Wanna try some?"

"Fuck no." She laughed. "Keep your mountain of gross to yourself."

"Your loss." He took another bite. "Now, how about you stop avoiding my question."

She grumbled as she kept at her ice cream. "He wasn't completely useless."

"Is that so?" He couldn't help the grin that pulled at his lip. She was sulking. He hadn't seen her sulk since he'd beat her on their tenth grade math test.

"He gave me a script for some fancy sleeping drugs." She pulled it out of the pocket of her jacket and showed it to him. She wanted to take the jacket off. It was irritating as hell, but she didn't want people staring at her. She hated people staring at her.

He looked at it skeptically. "Alice will want to see that."

"I'll show her whenever she finds us." She shoved it back into her pocket. "Assuming they are going to find us."

"I let her know we were here." He glanced around the crowded food court just to check that they hadn't wandered over yet. "Last I heard they were making serious life decisions about shoes."

"Well, shoes are pretty serious," she joked and had him choking on his ice cream.

"You own two pairs, Sparky. Runners and work boots."

"Not true," she challenged. "I have sandals and heels that Bea picked out."

"Fine, let me rephrase. You only wear two kinds of shoes."

She was going to shrug but thought better of it. "I'll give you that."

"Now, back to the topic at hand." He crunched into his cone. "How useful was Dr. Simms?"

"Define useful?" She was still licking at her ice cream and wondering how the hell he was already at the cone.

"Did you get anything out of the hour other than a script for sleeping pills?" He turned on his stool to face her as opposed to the crowd of people in the food court.

"I got a cup of coffee." She didn't meet his gaze but instead kept watching the people. She felt his hand on her arm.

"Cut the bullshit, Darcy." She glanced over at the harshness in his tone. "I just want to know you're okay. I want to know that we made the right choice today."

"Well, it didn't hurt going. At least, not once I was in there." She chewed on her bottom lip. "It wasn't terrible. But I don't really know what I was supposed to get out of it."

"I'm the wrong person to ask. I almost failed psychology in high school." He ran a hand through his hair. "Did he give you any advice?"

"Nope." She licked ice cream off her fingers. She'd forgotten about her cone long enough for it to begin melting. "We just talked. He wondered if I was a harm to myself though." She sent him a raised brow look. "What exactly has every one been gossiping about when I'm not around?"

He looked sheepish for a moment and stared at his hands now that they were free of ice cream. He didn't really know what to do with them now that they had nothing in them. "We were worried, darlin'."

"Your worrying hasn't done you so well in the past, Coop." She glanced down at his hands, lined with still healing marks from the fire.

He balled them into fists and tucked them into the pockets of his jacket. "What the hell was I supposed to do? Leave you there?"

"I don't know." She chewed on her bottom lip some more. "I just don't know about anything."

He watched the tears well up, so suddenly that they caught him off guard. They were already spilling over by the time he laid a hand on her cheek. "We'll get this sorted, Darcy. One way or another, we'll get everything back to normal."

"I don't know if we can get back there, Coop." She squeezed her eyes shut, hating the tears even as they continued to fall.

"Then we'll find a new normal." He offered a small smile. "We're good at that."

She nodded, not trusting herself to form words right now. Not trusting herself not to say something mean or terrible. So, she just nodded and cried and let her ice cream melt in her hand.

* * *

Alice liked shopping. When she went on her own it was often a rather mechanical experience that consisted of going in, grabbing what she wanted, and leaving. There was little joy in it. When she went with her sister and mother it was a whole different ball game. They could shop.

She had always known that. She'd grown up with it. But she had never found the time for it in her day-to-day life. So, she was enjoying this girl's day out even if she was a little distracted. Even if her mind was on Darcy and her appointment.

They had been to half the stores in the mall and all the stores that sold anything feminine. Alice had new shoes, new underwear, new shirts, and a new dress that she would need to find an occasion to wear. Her arms were full of bags, she had a coffee in one hand and a smile on her face as they left the shoe store. She was just debating whether they needed to venture to the lingerie store when her phone sounded from her pocket.

She cursed before she caught herself. Glancing back at her mother, who was still in conversation with Bea, she realized she hadn't been heard. She wrestled her phone out, almost dropped her coffee in the process, and managed to accept the call before it went to voicemail.

"Hello?"

"You owe me big time, McKnight."

She smiled as the voice floated through the phone to her. It was deep, male, and familiar. "Simms, I called in a favour. So, I think we're even."

"Not even close," he chuckled. "You undersold her completely. And now you need to pay up for it."

Alice heaved a sigh. She knew there was no negotiating with him. She'd given up trying to win arguments with shrinks a long time ago. "Tell me what you got out of the hour and I'll owe you a favour."

"I'm done with favours, McKnight. You owe me dinner before you run back off to the south."

"Dinner?" He couldn't be serious, she thought. But she could tell by his tone that he was exactly that.

"Dinner. Say yes and I'll fill you in."

She glanced over at her mother and Bea who were still chatting as they sat on a mall bench waiting for her. Alice knew she could say no. She knew she could request the file and be done with it. But that would take time. She didn't have time. She needed to know now what she was dealing with.

"Fine, dinner. Name the time and place and I'll be there." She tried not to grumble and kept the string of curses running mentally. "Now, tell me what I'm dealing with, Simms."

"I only had an hour with her but it's fairly classic trauma victim. Depression and hints of PTSD. Once the pain is managed she'll need to get that under control or she'll spiral. It's all a little much for her now. The pain, the insomnia, the life style changes – it's enough to derail anyone," he sighed. "I gave her a script for a sleep aid. It should help but it won't take away the nightmares."

"I'll see that it gets filled." Alice sipped her coffee absently.

"Please see that you do. The girl needs to sleep. She looks dead on her feet."

"I know." She wanted to snap. She wanted to say more. To ask him if he thought she hadn't noticed. But he had done her a favour and right now she was grateful for that. "Thank you, Simms. It really helps a lot."

"Anything for an old friend." His voice was sincere. "I'll follow up with you about dinner."

Alice hung up the phone without comment and slipped it back into her pocket. She didn't know what she was going to do about Darcy. But she knew that something had to be done. The girl was suffering. And she was causing herself most of the pain. Alice wondered if it was the curse of all stubborn people to be masochists. She hoped she never had to find out.

Plastering a smile on, she rejoined her mother and sister at the mall bench. She wanted to go to the lingerie store still. Hell, if they were there already she might as well get something nice. And despite her mother's modest upbringing, the woman was surprisingly good a picking out sexy clothes. Alice would never quite get used to it.

She followed them into the store, laughing with them and enjoying their company. She would file away what Simms had told her until later. Right now, she was going to enjoy the little bit of normalcy she had before it was back to work. Right now, she was just going to have some fun.

Chapter 34

The house was a frenzy of motion. Bags littered the kitchen table and their contents spilled over it. Coop had left the room, no doubt finding wherever his father was hiding and joining him. There was something about men and shopping that never seemed to mix.

Darcy stared at the bags. They had only been at the mall for a few hours. She didn't think it was physically possible for them to acquire this much stuff. Yet, there it all was in plain sight.

She sipped her coffee, seated a little away from the chaos on the kitchen counter. Bea was regaling her with stories about all of their amazing finds. Telling her about the people they had snatched items away from. The good deals they'd gotten.

Darcy listened with half an ear. It wasn't that she didn't like the stories. It wasn't that she didn't like looking at all the new stuff. It was just that her mind was still on her conversation with Coop. She was still trying to wrap her head around so many things that the simplicity of shopping was beyond her.

"I got you this dress." Bea held out a flowy summer dress in a light green. "I figured it would be great for the weather back home and that the thin straps wouldn't bother you so much."

"You didn't have to," Darcy muttered taking the dress and enjoying the soft, light feeling of the fabric.

"Oh, you know how I get. When I see something that I like I either have to buy it for me or for someone else. And I have way too many dresses already, so I figured it would be perfect for you." Bea sent her a smile.

"It's a great colour." Darcy smiled. Green was one of her favourite colours. It always looked good with her red hair and pale skin.

"I thought it would suit you." Evie came back into the kitchen. "The boys are hiding but they still have the nerve to ask for a snack."

"And you're just nice enough to make them one, I reckon." Bea slipped into her southern twang without a hitch.

"Well, they are my boys." Evie smiled. "Oh, it feels nice to be back home but damned if I didn't have a good time."

"I can tell." Darcy jumped off the counter and pawed through the bags. "It looks like you got quite the haul here."

"They're not all for me," she started and then shrugged. "Well, they're mostly for me. But I haven't been shopping in a coon's age. So, I figured I deserved it."

"Of course you do." Darcy sent her a smile. "You deserve anything that will make you happy."

"Well, that's sweet of you to say, Darcy." Evie walked over and gave her a kiss on the cheek. "So do you. Now, let Bea show you the rest of the things she got you."

"There are more things?" Darcy glanced over at the table, a little afraid.

"I have a bit of a problem," Bea confessed and had both of them laughing.

Evie watched them paw through the bags at the table. It was a scene she'd seen before, multiple times over the years. And every time Darcy had the same tension in her shoulders and the same uncertainty in her eyes. She was excited to see the things, excited to touch and try on, but at the same time she knew that she wasn't responsible for any of the things being given to her. There was guilt there.

Evie wondered if she would ever grow out of it. She'd watched Darcy grow up, but she had grown out of so few of the habits that had been concreted by her teenage years. She was outspoken. She was rude and abrasive. She often lost more friends than she made. But underneath it all she was insecure, she was shy, and she felt guilty about every favour anyone ever did for her.

She knew that she and Duncan tried a little too hard sometimes. Evie knew that. She knew that Darcy didn't need to be hand held through anything. And it was in her nature to fight against everything. Evie knew Darcy would be fine on her own but she also knew that no one needed to go through anything on their own.

She remembered when they had bought her a prom dress. She smiled at the memory even as Bea showed Darcy the heels she'd picked out. Darcy had been appalled and touched at the thought that someone would buy her the dress. She hadn't even planed on going to prom. She had been about to cancel her date when Evie had brought in the dress.

"You shouldn't have," Darcy had said and Evie knew she'd meant it.

"Every girl needs to have her prom." Evie had handed her the dress and told her the heels were upstairs. She'd almost been in tears until she'd run upstairs with the dress in hand.

Evie had sent her and Coop, with their respective dates, off with a smile and lots of pictures that evening. That was the last time she'd been able to buy clothes for the girl. The last time she'd been able to give her anything to put that smile on her face. She wanted to see that again. Wanted her to think of something other than the pain and the nightmares. Seeing her at the table with Bea, she knew that she'd accomplished at least that.

* * *

Coop found her in her room, which was surprising. He was so used to her being in his room, in his space that the idea of her back in her own scared him a little. He wasn't ready for her to go back to her space. He didn't think she was ready.

He thought about knocking on the doorjamb but dismissed it. They had moved passed knocking a long time ago. She had reminded him of that days ago. It shocked him that it had only been days ago. So much had happened in such a short amount of time. And yet, they still had a long way to go.

When he stepped into the room he found her on the bed, bags of clothing scattered around her. She was staring at a pair of black and silver heels as though they were the most fascinating objects on the planet. He'd seen that look on her face before, more than once. It never meant good things.

"You know you're supposed to wear those, not just stare at them," he commented, shoving his hands into his pockets. He didn't know what to do with them.

She held up a shoe, the look of confusion still on her face. "Do you know what this is?"

"A shoe?" He raised a brow.

"These shoes." She gestured with the one in her hand at its twin on the bed. "They are over two hundred dollars. I joked with Bea about them at Christmas." She glanced down at them, still a little shocked to see them in front of her. "It's a ridiculous amount to pay for footwear I told her and we laughed about it. And what does she do? Go out and buy them. What the hell do I need two hundred dollar shoes for?"

He shrugged. She looked so completely helpless staring at those shoes. He hated seeing her look helpless. "They're just shoes. Bea likes to give gifts."

"Your family is big on gifts," she mumbled setting the shoe down and running her hand over the cashmere sweater Evie had picked out. "They can't keep doing this, Coop. I can't keep getting hand-outs."

"Pretty sure mum would actually hit you for that comment." He ground his teeth together.

"You know I don't mean it like that, Coop." She ran a hand over her hair and looked at him for help. She found his brown eyes colder than usual.

"I honestly don't know what you mean, Darcy." He took his hands from his pockets and ran them over his face. He prayed for calm.

"I can take care of myself." She lifted her arms helplessly.

"No, you can't," he said it too sharply and saw her flinch at the words. "Have you not figured that out yet? You need us right now. As stubborn as you are, you need us until you get better." He ran both hands through his hair and tugged. "Why do you have to be so difficult?"

She shrugged. She wasn't used to him being mad at her. "It's just who I am?"

"I wish that wasn't true," he signed heavily. "But you don't have to turn away every favour people do, darlin'."

"I don't think two hundred dollar shoes count as a favour." She scowled at the shoes.

"Then tell Bea to take them back. Tell her you don't want them." He took a step towards her and the shoes and had to laugh when she hugged them close to her.

"No..." She looked at the shoes. "That would be rude."

"Yes, I'm sure she would take great offence to it." He sat down on the bed next to her and placed his hand over hers. "Are you alright, Sparky? I think this is about more than shoes."

"It so often is." She set them aside and gave his hand a squeeze. "But I think I'm just gonna take some of my meds and nap for a while." She offered him a smile. "Thanks for checking up on me, Coop."

He searched her bright eyes for something more, for whatever she wasn't saying but she was already closing herself off. So, he just nodded and left her to her nap. He'd try again later. Eventually, she would tell him what was going on. She always did.

Chapter 35

Darcy slipped out of bed as silently as she could. She didn't want to wake him and his soft snores assured her that he was still sleeping. She'd decided last night that she was leaving. She couldn't stay there any longer. She couldn't be a burden on his family any longer.

She knew that they wouldn't see it that way. They would never see her as a burden. The expression on Coop's face last night had been a clear indication of that. But she felt like she was causing more pain than good lately. Family members were fighting over her, people were taking time for her, and they were spending money on her. She hated that it came down to money, but that had always been a division between herself and the McKnights.

She loved them, like they were her own family. But the truth was that they weren't. Her family had been poor and struggling. She'd grown up in a cramped apartment that was often either too cold or too warm. The walls had been thin, the rent was mostly paid on time, and her mama had worked herself to death to keep them there. She had stayed with the McKnights. She had experienced their type of living. But it didn't belong to her and she would never take advantage of it.

She had done alright on her own. Racing had given her an income that her family had never had. She had money that she didn't even know how to spend because she'd never grown up being frivolous and still they spoiled her. But she would not take advantage of that generosity, no matter how freely they offered it.

She'd tossed her clothes in a bag after dinner. She intentionally left all of the new things Bea had gotten her in the room upstairs. She would take only what belonged to her. She knew it was rude to reject the gifts but it didn't feel right taking them right now. She didn't want them. She didn't want anything else from them at the moment. She just wanted to get away.

Coop had been busy in the garage and hadn't noticed her slip away to pack. Now, all she had to do was slip out of the bedroom, grab the bag she had stashed, and leave through the patio doors. By the time they woke up in the morning she would be miles away.

Coop would be pissed. First, because she was gone and second, because she was taking his bike. But she had written a note. He would find it and hopefully he would understand that this was something she needed to do. And hopefully he wouldn't come looking for her. She knew that it was a naïve belief, but it was all she had.

If she left then Alice would go back to work. And he could go back to the garage in Senoia and pick up where he'd been headed before she'd convinced him to run off with her. They could all have a normal life. They could all move on with their lives and stop worrying about her. Because worrying about her got people hurt.

She would just go take care of herself. She had been doing that for most of her life anyhow. She didn't know where she was going, but when she got there she would know. And they would be free and clear of her.

She had never felt like running away before in her life. She had never wanted to leave the McKnights. But she felt as though she was tearing their family apart and she couldn't live with that. She couldn't be the reason for that. She'd been responsible for enough anger and violence in her life. She would not bring that into the one family she did love.

"And where do you think you're going?"

She'd made it to the door before his voice stopped her. She didn't want to turn around. She couldn't bring herself to see the potential suspicion, anger, or worse, hurt, in his eyes. So instead, she replied to the door rather than face him. "Bathroom. I'll be back."

"Bullshit." He clicked on the bedside lamp and swung out of bed. Her voice was far from steady but even if it had been, he would have heard the lie in the few words.

"Pardon?" She turned to face him now; more shocked by how he spat out the word than anything else, and watched him tug his jeans on over the boxers he'd been wearing.

"You never were very good at lying, darlin'." He didn't look at her as he tugged the shirt over his head. "At least, not to me."

"I was..." she found the words died in her mouth. He wasn't looking at her. He was just sitting there staring at the wall and somehow that was worse than if he'd been staring at her angrily. She wished he would look at her so she could figure out what emotion was hiding behind those words.

"You were running off." He flexed his hands and resisted the urge to ball them into fists. He was angry, more at himself than at her. Because he should have known from the look in her eyes last night that she was planning this. He should have known her well enough to be prepared for it. "You were just gonna steal off in the night without so much as a word."

"I was leavin' a note," she said lamely. She couldn't resist staring down at her feet.

He chuckled humourlessly. "I'm sure you put a great deal of thought into that too."

She shuffled her feet. She didn't know what to do when he wouldn't look at her. She couldn't see what he was feeling. "I can't keep doing this to you, Coop. I can't do this to your family. It's too much."

"No one likes a damn martyr, Darcy." He glanced at her then and she saw not anger in those brown eyes but hurt.

"I can't be a burden on your family anymore. I won't be." She didn't know what to do with the emotion in his eyes. She could deal with him angry. She had several times in the past. But she'd never seen him look at her like this.

"And what about me?" He rose from the bed, but didn't go to her. He didn't trust himself to. "You were just going to leave me here. Wondering where the hell you went. Do I mean so little to you?"

That hurt. She felt the sting of the words as he said them and began to understand the pain in his eyes. "You mean everything to me, Coop. You're my best friend."

He bit back the words that wanted to spill out. He wanted to yell at her. He wanted to scream and throw things. But he knew that anger would get him nowhere with her. He'd tried that before.

So, he went a different route. "Then don't leave," he said, voice soft.

She shook her head. She didn't know if she could answer him. She suddenly felt very useless standing there, one hand on the doorknob, looking at him. What on earth had she been thinking?

"Then let me come with you." Coop crossed to her now and laid a hand on her arm. He kept his touch gentle even though he wanted to grab her and shake her for being so stupid. He knew she would resist the anger. She was stubborn like that. But he could win her over if he tried other methods.

"If you want to leave so badly then we'll go." He met her gaze, his eyes sincere. "I'll toss some things in a bag and we'll hit the road. But you aren't leaving without me."

"Coop..." Her eyes pleaded with him. Why couldn't he understand? Why didn't he see that this was the problem? "Your family..."

"You're my family, damnit!" He let go of her arm before his hand could tighten around it. "When will you get that through your thick skull."

She'd just wanted to sneak away. But she knew that there was no hope of that anymore. She searched his face and saw the familiar determined lines. She saw the anger floating underneath the hurt. There was no way she was leaving the Basin alone.

"You have fifteen minutes to get your stuff together or I'm leavin' without you." She turned the doorknob and pulled it open. Her anger was bubbling to the surface now, fuelled by his stubbornness. "And Coop, you're my family too. The only one I've got."

She closed the door behind her. She resisted the urge to lean against it. Her pain was manageable at the moment and the action would have put her over the edge. Instead, she grabbed her bag from its hiding place and settled down on the couch to wait. She would give him the fifteen minutes. But that was all she would give him.

Coop was out of his room in ten. It had taken him less than five to pack what he'd needed but he'd spent the rest of the time scribbling a note to Alice. He knew she would try to call him when she found it, but he wasn't certain if he would answer just yet.

Still, he wanted her to know that he was with Darcy. He wanted her to know that he would take care of her and make sure she took her meds. He wanted her to understand that this was what they needed to do. At least, as much as he could manage to do in a one page note.

They went outside in silence. Neither of them completely happy with the current situation. She'd shrugged into her jacket and it was only mildly irritating. He was wearing his scarred leather jacket that looked like it belonged on him. He handed her his second helmet and swung onto the Rebel.

"Where to?" He glanced back at her.

"Let's go home," she answered strapping the helmet on and stowing her bag in the saddlebags on the side. "But let's take the scenic route."

"Sure thing, darlin'." Coop tossed her his own bag before swinging into his seat. He kicked the motorcycle to life and enjoyed the sound of the engine underneath him. He felt her arms wrap around him and the smile pulled at his lips. It might not be the best solution, he thought as they pulled out of the drive but it was what they had at the moment.

At least she wasn't alone. As long as he had any say in it she never would be. That was the one thing he could guarantee.

ABOUT THE AUTHOR

S.G. Reid grew up in Bancroft, Ontario and has spent most of her life in small Ontarian towns. This sparked a curiosity about small towns and rural living, for small-town dynamics and eccentricities. She incorporates these aspects into her writing as often as possible.

She holds a Masters Degree in Criminology but her passion has always been for writing, a passion that she has pursued for over a decade.

Sneak Preview of Rise from the Ashes

Welcome, race fans! It's that time again and I can tell ya'll have been waitin' all winter for it. Can ya tell me just how excited ya'll are?

Darcy listened to the crowd roar, the smile tugging at her lips reluctantly. It was a different type of excitement that worked its way through her system right now. It wasn't the hand-shaking nerves that she had before each series race. This was different. This was familiar.

The Senoia Speedway was the first track she'd ever raced on. The first real track anyway. This was the only track that had ever caused her to throw up before a race. The track she'd made her name on.

No, this wasn't the same excitement. This was more like coming home.

We have a special guest for ya'll tonight. She'll be sneaking into the race, but I don't think ya'll will be too mad about it. Give a warm welcome to our local celebrity, Darcy van Dyke!

She listened to the crowd cheer at her name. Felt the energy in it. There was something there. Something that was missing from the big stadium stands of the series. This was real care. It went beyond the fan worship that existed on the circuit. These stands were filled with neighbours, parents, siblings, cousins, friends, and co-workers. Everyone in the county came out for the first race of the season. That was why her sponsor had wanted her to come out for it.

Good marketing, he'd said in his slimy, used car-salesman's voice. She had never much cared for the man, but sponsors were hard to come by. A little bit of money here and there helped, especially when racing stock cars at the track. But when moving up to the series it took a lot more than small change to make things happen. She'd needed a real sponsor and a car. Cooper had found both. That didn't mean she needed to like the sponsor.

She glanced over at her stock car. She'd borrowed it from James Gillis or Gilly to anyone who knew him. He was out of the race due to a broken leg. A non-racing related injury, according to his wife, who claimed he'd fallen off a ladder while fixing the roof. It was a shame he couldn't race but she was glad that the car had been available. Her stock car had been sold off long ago.

It wasn't a perfect fit. She missed her old car. But her and Coop had spent months making that thing perfect. Days spent in the garage welding and wiring and painting. It had been made for her. This wasn't hers. But she didn't need to win today. She just needed to put on a show.

She gave Coop a smile as he retrieved her helmet. "They're a rowdy bunch tonight."

He ran a hand through his shaggy hair, a big grin on his face. "Yeah, it's great, ain't it?"

He glanced down at her. It was different seeing her in the loose coveralls as opposed to the fitted series uniform. She still had the sponsors sewed on, they'd made sure of that, but with less care than her pristine race suit. There was a familiarity to her current look, even if it was different. "They always were excited for the first race of the season."

"They live for it." She juggled her helmet from one arm to another. "The car all set?"

He glanced at the stock car, his eyes shifting from humourous to critical. "It was nice of Gilly to let ya use his car." He gave a half shrug. "It's not great, but it's sound." He sent her a grin. "With a month I could make her win every race no matter who drove her."

"You always thought the driver had little to do with it."

"Well, maybe a little." He reached over to ruffle her hair but she ducked out of the way. "You ready to do this?"

"Like riding a bike, right?" She piled her hair atop her head in a one-handed twist before shoving her helmet on. "I know every inch of this track."

"Now who's being cocky, Sparky?" He shouted but she was already sliding into the car as the announcer called all drivers to the track.

He hadn't been nearly as reluctant as her to come back to the old track. As great as the IndyCar series had been, there were so many rules. Stock car racing left more room for invention. He'd always liked the loopholes and the corners that could be skated around. Sure there were standards still, but they were more basic on the dirt track. Everything was simpler on the dirt track.

He'd gone over Gilly's car carefully. Just because a car passed general inspection didn't mean that it was completely track worthy. He wasn't about to put her in anything that wasn't one-hundred percent safe to go on the track. It didn't matter what track she was racing on.

He'd fought his way to head mechanic of her pit team in the series. He'd strong-armed the owner. He'd proven his worth. And she never went on the track without his seal of approval. He took that responsibility seriously.

He watched her stock car, number 87, pull into line with the others. She wasn't in a good position but she was an add-in. It would have been unfair to the others; the seasoned racers who needed the prize money to feed their families or repair their cars. Some people took racing seriously. Some people did it as a job.

He thought of Darcy. She had never intended it to be a job. He was sure of that. He remembered her in high school. She'd had all these plans. None of them had included racing stock cars or Indy cars. But life often tossed you in strange directions, he mused. He couldn't picture her doing anything else now.

He watched the car round the first lap with the rest of them. Warming up and showing off. The audience was on their feet with signs in support of their favourite cars. People clapped and screamed and blew horns. It was the atmosphere he enjoyed. There was something honest about it.

"She ready for this?"

Coop glanced back at Kevin McAllister, owner of McAllister Industries. Coop still didn't fully understand what the company did. But the man had money. And he wanted that money to go into racing, so that was just fine. And from the little Coop did understand, his company dealt with pharmaceuticals. Why the man wanted anything to do with racing Coop had no clue. But if he wanted his logo splayed across their hood, Coop was happy to oblige.

"She's always ready for a race." Coop turned his attention back to the track as the green flag waved and they were off. "Now, why don't you go sit in the stands, Kevin," he said dismissively. "We've got work to do."

"That's my racer out there!" Kevin called out but Coop was already walking away, slipping his headset on as he went.

He smiled as he spoke into the mouthpiece. "How you doin' out there, Sparky?"

Darcy heard his voice come through the headset she wore underneath her helmet. She grinned even as she passed the car in front of her on turn two. "I forgot how much give the dirt track has."

"They watered it down pretty good before ya'll got out there, but it'll hopefully dry out in a few laps." He watched her carefully as she rounded her eighth lap. The quarter mile track was hardly a challenge, but the tight corners and the wet dirt could pose a problem.

She was out of practice on a dirt track and it was a congested race with over fifty drivers. But there were plenty of laps to go in the fifty-lap race. And he expected the number of drivers would go down by a third before they hit the halfway point.

She was moving up nicely. Passing on the inside on the turns. Not pressing her advantage and staying out of any money positions. She wouldn't take the prize from anyone but she also wouldn't settle for crossing the finish line out of the top ten. After all, she had a reputation to keep.

The car drove well. She would give Coop and Gilly that. It still wasn't her car but she was happy with the way it handled. She'd forgotten what it was like to drive on the dirt. She'd forgotten how it pulled at her wheels. How the corners tugged her towards the outside if she didn't fight the wheel. It was a struggle compared to a paved track and she loved every minute of it.

"Halfway point, Sparky." Coop's voice flowed through her headset. "How you holdin' up out there?"

"Few bumps and bruises, but no harm done," she said with a laugh.

"The other guys are really ridin' you out there," he chuckled.

"They've got something to prove." She would have shrugged if he could have seen it. "I'm just here for the show."

She pulled up next to car 99 and slipped around him on turn three. The move put her in seventh place and she was more than happy with the spot.

"Dan's not too happy you cut him off."

"That was Dan?" She thought of the clean-cut guy they'd gone to school with and it was her turn to laugh. "Well, I'll buy him a beer after the race and maybe he'll calm down."

"Keep an eye on him, Sparky." Coop's voice held a tone of warning. "He seems pretty set on getting by you."

"Let him try," she muttered but still shot a glance back at him. He was closer than she would have liked and she definitely didn't appreciate how he was bumping into her back end every time he got closer.

She took the third turn higher than she wanted to. The dirt pulling her towards the barrier. She cursed as she fought with the wheel to pull the car back to the inside of curve. Even as Dan tried to cut passed her on the inside.

Coop watched it from the pits. It took seconds, but that was all it ever took. The 99 car clipped her rear, driver's side panel and sent her spinning. Then the wheel caught and the car flipped.

He was over the barrier before anyone to grab his arm to

stop him. He had to wait for the wave of cars to pass before sprinting across the track but the seconds that took weighed on him. Her car was still upside down and she wasn't getting out of it.

The caution flag had waved and the cars were circling at a crawl. He could see the emergency vehicle crossing from the pits out of the corner of his eyes, but it still had a distance to travel.

He felt the dread rush through him before he even saw the flames. They were creeping through the mesh over the rear windows and licking their way up the body. The gas tank in the back would explode if they didn't put it out. Even if it did, he'd still have time to get her out. The flash of it would be brutal, but it would subside. He could get her out.

He heard her scream just before it exploded. He knew he should have stopped. He knew he should have waited. But there was no time. He closed the distance, sliding across the dirt towards the car.

Smoke was billowing from the back of the car. Fire was making its way to the front. Darcy was struggling to keep herself in her seat with one hand while fighting with her harness with the other.

Her eyes met his through the clouded plastic of her helmet visor and he read the terror in them. He saw the pain in them.

He fumbled for the multi-tool in his pocket. The one that was always there. Flipping open the blade, he sliced the harness, not even noticing the flames the licked at his hands as he worked.

She didn't have time to brace herself before falling against the roof of the car. She'd barely touched it before he was dragging her out the window and across the dirt. Away from the car. Away from the fire.

"I got you. You're safe."

She heard his voice, but barely.

Coop watched the emergency vehicle reach the car. What had felt like hours had been mere seconds. Half the crew set to work extinguishing the flames while two medics ran over to them.

Coop felt himself shaking his head as they shouted questions at him. "Help her. She's the one who needs it."

"Your hands."

He glanced down at his hands for the first time. Registering the pain that was radiating from them up his arms. He flexed them experimentally and cursed. He sent the medic a nod, realizing it was useless to argue.

He had gotten her out. She was safe. But even as he looked at her laid out on the stretcher, he knew he hadn't been quick enough. And he knew he'd have to live with that for the rest of his life.

Made in the USA
Middletown, DE
24 September 2020